Wi

## Dramatis Personae

King Henry the Fourth.
Henry, Prince of Wales, son to the King.
Prince John of Lancaster, son to the King.
Earl of Westmoreland.
Sir Walter Blunt.
Thomas Percy, Earl of Worcester.
Henry Percy, Earl of Northumberland.
Henry Percy, his son.
Edmund Mortimer, Earl of March.
Scroop, Archbishop of York.
Sir Michael, his Friend.
Archibald, Earl of Douglas.
Owen Glendower.
Sir Richard Vernon.
Sir John Falstaff.
Pointz.
Gadshill.
Peto.
Bardolph.
Lady Percy, Wife to Hotspur.
Lady Mortimer, Daughter to Glendower.
Mrs. Quickly, Hostess in Eastcheap.
Lords, Officers, Sheriff, Vintner, Chamberlain, Drawers,
Carriers, Travellers, and Attendants.

## ACT I

### SCENE I. London. The palace.

*Enter KING HENRY, LORD JOHN OF LANCASTER, the EARL of WESTMORELAND, SIR WALTER BLUNT, and others*

**KING HENRY IV**

So shaken as we are, so wan with care,
Find we a time for frighted peace to pant,
And breathe short-winded accents of new broils
To be commenced in strands afar remote.
No more the thirsty entrance of this soil
Shall daub her lips with her own children's blood;
Nor more shall trenching war channel her fields,
Nor bruise her flowerets with the armed hoofs
Of hostile paces: those opposed eyes,
Which, like the meteors of a troubled heaven,
All of one nature, of one substance bred,
Did lately meet in the intestine shock
And furious close of civil butchery
Shall now, in mutual well-beseeming ranks,
March all one way and be no more opposed
Against acquaintance, kindred and allies:
The edge of war, like an ill-sheathed knife,
No more shall cut his master. Therefore, friends,
As far as to the sepulchre of Christ,
Whose soldier now, under whose blessed cross
We are impressed and engaged to fight,
Forthwith a power of English shall we levy;
Whose arms were moulded in their mothers' womb
To chase these pagans in those holy fields
Over whose acres walk'd those blessed feet
Which fourteen hundred years ago were nail'd
For our advantage on the bitter cross.
But this our purpose now is twelve month old,
And bootless 'tis to tell you we will go:
Therefore we meet not now. Then let me hear
Of you, my gentle cousin Westmoreland,
What yesternight our council did decree
In forwarding this dear expedience.

**WESTMORELAND**

My liege, this haste was hot in question,
And many limits of the charge set down
But yesternight: when all athwart there came
A post from Wales loaden with heavy news;
Whose worst was, that the noble Mortimer,
Leading the men of Herefordshire to fight
Against the irregular and wild Glendower,
Was by the rude hands of that Welshman taken,
A thousand of his people butchered;
Upon whose dead corpse there was such misuse,
Such beastly shameless transformation,
By those Welshwomen done as may not be
Without much shame retold or spoken of.

**KING HENRY IV**

It seems then that the tidings of this broil
Brake off our business for the Holy Land.

**WESTMORELAND**

This match'd with other did, my gracious lord;
For more uneven and unwelcome news
Came from the north and thus it did import:
On Holy-rood day, the gallant Hotspur there,
Young Harry Percy and brave Archibald,
That ever-valiant and approved Scot,
At Holmedon met,
Where they did spend a sad and bloody hour,

As by discharge of their artillery,
And shape of likelihood, the news was told;
For he that brought them, in the very heat
And pride of their contention did take horse,
Uncertain of the issue any way.

**KING HENRY IV**

Here is a dear, a true industrious friend,
Sir Walter Blunt, new lighted from his horse.
Stain'd with the variation of each soil
Betwixt that Holmedon and this seat of ours;
And he hath brought us smooth and welcome news.
The Earl of Douglas is discomfited:
Ten thousand bold Scots, two and twenty knights,
Balk'd in their own blood did Sir Walter see
On Holmedon's plains. Of prisoners, Hotspur took
Mordake the Earl of Fife, and eldest son
To beaten Douglas; and the Earl of Athol,
Of Murray, Angus, and Menteith:
And is not this an honourable spoil?
A gallant prize? ha, cousin, is it not?

**WESTMORELAND**

In faith,
It is a conquest for a prince to boast of.

**KING HENRY IV**

Yea, there thou makest me sad and makest me sin
In envy that my Lord Northumberland
Should be the father to so blest a son,
A son who is the theme of honour's tongue;
Amongst a grove, the very straightest plant;
Who is sweet Fortune's minion and her pride:
Whilst I, by looking on the praise of him,
See riot and dishonour stain the brow
Of my young Harry. O that it could be proved
That some night-tripping fairy had exchanged
In cradle-clothes our children where they lay,
And call'd mine Percy, his Plantagenet!
Then would I have his Harry, and he mine.
But let him from my thoughts. What think you, coz,
Of this young Percy's pride? the prisoners,
Which he in this adventure hath surprised,
To his own use he keeps; and sends me word,
I shall have none but Mordake Earl of Fife.

**WESTMORELAND**

This is his uncle's teaching; this is Worcester,
Malevolent to you in all aspects;
Which makes him prune himself, and bristle up
The crest of youth against your dignity.

**KING HENRY IV**

But I have sent for him to answer this;
And for this cause awhile we must neglect
Our holy purpose to Jerusalem.
Cousin, on Wednesday next our council we
Will hold at Windsor; so inform the lords:
But come yourself with speed to us again;
For more is to be said and to be done
Than out of anger can be uttered.

**WESTMORELAND**

I will, my liege.

*Exeunt*

**SCENE II. London. An apartment of the Prince's.**

*Enter the PRINCE OF WALES and FALSTAFF*

**FALSTAFF**

Now, Hal, what time of day is it, lad?

**PRINCE HENRY**
Thou art so fat-witted, with drinking of old sack
and unbuttoning thee after supper and sleeping upon
benches after noon, that thou hast forgotten to
demand that truly which thou wouldst truly know.
What a devil hast thou to do with the time of the
day? Unless hours were cups of sack and minutes
capons and clocks the tongues of bawds and dials the
signs of leaping-houses and the blessed sun himself
a fair hot wench in flame-coloured taffeta, I see no
reason why thou shouldst be so superfluous to demand
the time of the day.
**FALSTAFF**
Indeed, you come near me now, Hal; for we that take
purses go by the moon and the seven stars, and not
by Phoebus, he,'that wandering knight so fair.' And,
I prithee, sweet wag, when thou art king, as, God
save thy grace,--majesty I should say, for grace
thou wilt have none,--
**PRINCE HENRY**
What, none?
**FALSTAFF**
No, by my troth, not so much as will serve to
prologue to an egg and butter.
**PRINCE HENRY**
Well, how then? come, roundly, roundly.
**FALSTAFF**
Marry, then, sweet wag, when thou art king, let not
us that are squires of the night's body be called
thieves of the day's beauty: let us be Diana's
foresters, gentlemen of the shade, minions of the
moon; and let men say we be men of good government,
being governed, as the sea is, by our noble and
chaste mistress the moon, under whose countenance we steal.
**PRINCE HENRY**
Thou sayest well, and it holds well too; for the
fortune of us that are the moon's men doth ebb and
flow like the sea, being governed, as the sea is,
by the moon. As, for proof, now: a purse of gold
most resolutely snatched on Monday night and most
dissolutely spent on Tuesday morning; got with
swearing 'Lay by' and spent with crying 'Bring in;'
now in as low an ebb as the foot of the ladder
and by and by in as high a flow as the ridge of the gallows.
**FALSTAFF**
By the Lord, thou sayest true, lad. And is not my
hostess of the tavern a most sweet wench?
**PRINCE HENRY**
As the honey of Hybla, my old lad of the castle. And
is not a buff jerkin a most sweet robe of durance?
**FALSTAFF**
How now, how now, mad wag! what, in thy quips and
thy quiddities? what a plague have I to do with a
buff jerkin?
**PRINCE HENRY**
Why, what a pox have I to do with my hostess of the tavern?
**FALSTAFF**
Well, thou hast called her to a reckoning many a
time and oft.
**PRINCE HENRY**
Did I ever call for thee to pay thy part?
**FALSTAFF**
No; I'll give thee thy due, thou hast paid all there.

**PRINCE HENRY**
Yea, and elsewhere, so far as my coin would stretch;
and where it would not, I have used my credit.
**FALSTAFF**
Yea, and so used it that were it not here apparent
that thou art heir apparent--But, I prithee, sweet
wag, shall there be gallows standing in England when
thou art king? and resolution thus fobbed as it is
with the rusty curb of old father antic the law? Do
not thou, when thou art king, hang a thief.
**PRINCE HENRY**
No; thou shalt.
**FALSTAFF**
Shall I? O rare! By the Lord, I'll be a brave judge.
**PRINCE HENRY**
Thou judgest false already: I mean, thou shalt have
the hanging of the thieves and so become a rare hangman.
**FALSTAFF**
Well, Hal, well; and in some sort it jumps with my
humour as well as waiting in the court, I can tell
you.
**PRINCE HENRY**
For obtaining of suits?
**FALSTAFF**
Yea, for obtaining of suits, whereof the hangman
hath no lean wardrobe. 'Sblood, I am as melancholy
as a gib cat or a lugged bear.
**PRINCE HENRY**
Or an old lion, or a lover's lute.
**FALSTAFF**
Yea, or the drone of a Lincolnshire bagpipe.
**PRINCE HENRY**
What sayest thou to a hare, or the melancholy of
Moor-ditch?
**FALSTAFF**
Thou hast the most unsavoury similes and art indeed
the most comparative, rascalliest, sweet young
prince. But, Hal, I prithee, trouble me no more
with vanity. I would to God thou and I knew where a
commodity of good names were to be bought. An old
lord of the council rated me the other day in the
street about you, sir, but I marked him not; and yet
he talked very wisely, but I regarded him not; and
yet he talked wisely, and in the street too.
**PRINCE HENRY**
Thou didst well; for wisdom cries out in the
streets, and no man regards it.
**FALSTAFF**
O, thou hast damnable iteration and art indeed able
to corrupt a saint. Thou hast done much harm upon
me, Hal; God forgive thee for it! Before I knew
thee, Hal, I knew nothing; and now am I, if a man
should speak truly, little better than one of the
wicked. I must give over this life, and I will give
it over: by the Lord, and I do not, I am a villain:
I'll be damned for never a king's son in
Christendom.
**PRINCE HENRY**
Where shall we take a purse tomorrow, Jack?
**FALSTAFF**
'Zounds, where thou wilt, lad; I'll make one; an I
do not, call me villain and baffle me.
**PRINCE HENRY**

I see a good amendment of life in thee; from praying
to purse-taking.

**FALSTAFF**

Why, Hal, 'tis my vocation, Hal; 'tis no sin for a
man to labour in his vocation.

*Enter POINS*

Poins! Now shall we know if Gadshill have set a
match. O, if men were to be saved by merit, what
hole in hell were hot enough for him? This is the
most omnipotent villain that ever cried 'Stand' to
a true man.

**PRINCE HENRY**

Good morrow, Ned.

**POINS**

Good morrow, sweet Hal. What says Monsieur Remorse?
what says Sir John Sack and Sugar? Jack! how
agrees the devil and thee about thy soul, that thou
soldest him on Good-Friday last for a cup of Madeira
and a cold capon's leg?

**PRINCE HENRY**

Sir John stands to his word, the devil shall have
his bargain; for he was never yet a breaker of
proverbs: he will give the devil his due.

**POINS**

Then art thou damned for keeping thy word with the devil.

**PRINCE HENRY**

Else he had been damned for cozening the devil.

**POINS**

But, my lads, my lads, to-morrow morning, by four
o'clock, early at Gadshill! there are pilgrims going
to Canterbury with rich offerings, and traders
riding to London with fat purses: I have vizards
for you all; you have horses for yourselves:
Gadshill lies to-night in Rochester: I have bespoke
supper to-morrow night in Eastcheap: we may do it
as secure as sleep. If you will go, I will stuff
your purses full of crowns; if you will not, tarry
at home and be hanged.

**FALSTAFF**

Hear ye, Yedward; if I tarry at home and go not,
I'll hang you for going.

**POINS**

You will, chops?

**FALSTAFF**

Hal, wilt thou make one?

**PRINCE HENRY**

Who, I rob? I a thief? not I, by my faith.

**FALSTAFF**

There's neither honesty, manhood, nor good
fellowship in thee, nor thou camest not of the blood
royal, if thou darest not stand for ten shillings.

**PRINCE HENRY**

Well then, once in my days I'll be a madcap.

**FALSTAFF**

Why, that's well said.

**PRINCE HENRY**

Well, come what will, I'll tarry at home.

**FALSTAFF**

By the Lord, I'll be a traitor then, when thou art king.

**PRINCE HENRY**

I care not.

**POINS**

Sir John, I prithee, leave the prince and me alone:
I will lay him down such reasons for this adventure
that he shall go.

**FALSTAFF**

Well, God give thee the spirit of persuasion and him
the ears of profiting, that what thou speakest may
move and what he hears may be believed, that the
true prince may, for recreation sake, prove a false
thief; for the poor abuses of the time want
countenance. Farewell: you shall find me in Eastcheap.

**PRINCE HENRY**

Farewell, thou latter spring! farewell, All-hallown summer!

*Exit Falstaff*

**POINS**

Now, my good sweet honey lord, ride with us
to-morrow: I have a jest to execute that I cannot
manage alone. Falstaff, Bardolph, Peto and Gadshill
shall rob those men that we have already waylaid:
yourself and I will not be there; and when they
have the booty, if you and I do not rob them, cut
this head off from my shoulders.

**PRINCE HENRY**

How shall we part with them in setting forth?

**POINS**

Why, we will set forth before or after them, and
appoint them a place of meeting, wherein it is at
our pleasure to fail, and then will they adventure
upon the exploit themselves; which they shall have
no sooner achieved, but we'll set upon them.

**PRINCE HENRY**

Yea, but 'tis like that they will know us by our
horses, by our habits and by every other
appointment, to be ourselves.

**POINS**

Tut! our horses they shall not see: I'll tie them
in the wood; our vizards we will change after we
leave them: and, sirrah, I have cases of buckram
for the nonce, to immask our noted outward garments.

**PRINCE HENRY**

Yea, but I doubt they will be too hard for us.

**POINS**

Well, for two of them, I know them to be as
true-bred cowards as ever turned back; and for the
third, if he fight longer than he sees reason, I'll
forswear arms. The virtue of this jest will be, the
incomprehensible lies that this same fat rogue will
tell us when we meet at supper: how thirty, at
least, he fought with; what wards, what blows, what
extremities he endured; and in the reproof of this
lies the jest.

**PRINCE HENRY**

Well, I'll go with thee: provide us all things
necessary and meet me to-morrow night in Eastcheap;
there I'll sup. Farewell.

**POINS**

Farewell, my lord.

*Exit Poins*

**PRINCE HENRY**

I know you all, and will awhile uphold
The unyoked humour of your idleness:
Yet herein will I imitate the sun,
Who doth permit the base contagious clouds
To smother up his beauty from the world,

That, when he please again to be himself,
Being wanted, he may be more wonder'd at,
By breaking through the foul and ugly mists
Of vapours that did seem to strangle him.
If all the year were playing holidays,
To sport would be as tedious as to work;
But when they seldom come, they wish'd for come,
And nothing pleaseth but rare accidents.
So, when this loose behavior I throw off
And pay the debt I never promised,
By how much better than my word I am,
By so much shall I falsify men's hopes;
And like bright metal on a sullen ground,
My reformation, glittering o'er my fault,
Shall show more goodly and attract more eyes
Than that which hath no foil to set it off.
I'll so offend, to make offence a skill;
Redeeming time when men think least I will.
*Exit*
**SCENE III. London. The palace.**
*Enter the KING, NORTHUMBERLAND, WORCESTER, HOTSPUR, SIR WALTER BLUNT, with others*
**KING HENRY IV**
My blood hath been too cold and temperate,
Unapt to stir at these indignities,
And you have found me; for accordingly
You tread upon my patience: but be sure
I will from henceforth rather be myself,
Mighty and to be fear'd, than my condition;
Which hath been smooth as oil, soft as young down,
And therefore lost that title of respect
Which the proud soul ne'er pays but to the proud.
**EARL OF WORCESTER**
Our house, my sovereign liege, little deserves
The scourge of greatness to be used on it;
And that same greatness too which our own hands
Have holp to make so portly.
**NORTHUMBERLAND**
My lord.--
**KING HENRY IV**
Worcester, get thee gone; for I do see
Danger and disobedience in thine eye:
O, sir, your presence is too bold and peremptory,
And majesty might never yet endure
The moody frontier of a servant brow.
You have good leave to leave us: when we need
Your use and counsel, we shall send for you.
*Exit Worcester*
You were about to speak.
*To North*
**NORTHUMBERLAND**
Yea, my good lord.
Those prisoners in your highness' name demanded,
Which Harry Percy here at Holmedon took,
Were, as he says, not with such strength denied
As is deliver'd to your majesty:
Either envy, therefore, or misprison
Is guilty of this fault and not my son.
**HOTSPUR**
My liege, I did deny no prisoners.
But I remember, when the fight was done,
When I was dry with rage and extreme toil,
Breathless and faint, leaning upon my sword,

Came there a certain lord, neat, and trimly dress'd,
Fresh as a bridegroom; and his chin new reap'd
Show'd like a stubble-land at harvest-home;
He was perfumed like a milliner;
And 'twixt his finger and his thumb he held
A pouncet-box, which ever and anon
He gave his nose and took't away again;
Who therewith angry, when it next came there,
Took it in snuff; and still he smiled and talk'd,
And as the soldiers bore dead bodies by,
He call'd them untaught knaves, unmannerly,
To bring a slovenly unhandsome corse
Betwixt the wind and his nobility.
With many holiday and lady terms
He question'd me; amongst the rest, demanded
My prisoners in your majesty's behalf.
I then, all smarting with my wounds being cold,
To be so pester'd with a popinjay,
Out of my grief and my impatience,
Answer'd neglectingly I know not what,
He should or he should not; for he made me mad
To see him shine so brisk and smell so sweet
And talk so like a waiting-gentlewoman
Of guns and drums and wounds,--God save the mark!--
And telling me the sovereign'st thing on earth
Was parmaceti for an inward bruise;
And that it was great pity, so it was,
This villanous salt-petre should be digg'd
Out of the bowels of the harmless earth,
Which many a good tall fellow had destroy'd
So cowardly; and but for these vile guns,
He would himself have been a soldier.
This bald unjointed chat of his, my lord,
I answer'd indirectly, as I said;
And I beseech you, let not his report
Come current for an accusation
Betwixt my love and your high majesty.
**SIR WALTER BLUNT**
The circumstance consider'd, good my lord,
Whate'er Lord Harry Percy then had said
To such a person and in such a place,
At such a time, with all the rest retold,
May reasonably die and never rise
To do him wrong or any way impeach
What then he said, so he unsay it now.
**KING HENRY IV**
Why, yet he doth deny his prisoners,
But with proviso and exception,
That we at our own charge shall ransom straight
His brother-in-law, the foolish Mortimer;
Who, on my soul, hath wilfully betray'd
The lives of those that he did lead to fight
Against that great magician, damn'd Glendower,
Whose daughter, as we hear, the Earl of March
Hath lately married. Shall our coffers, then,
Be emptied to redeem a traitor home?
Shall we but treason? and indent with fears,
When they have lost and forfeited themselves?
No, on the barren mountains let him starve;
For I shall never hold that man my friend
Whose tongue shall ask me for one penny cost
To ransom home revolted Mortimer.
**HOTSPUR**

Revolted Mortimer!
He never did fall off, my sovereign liege,
But by the chance of war; to prove that true
Needs no more but one tongue for all those wounds,
Those mouthed wounds, which valiantly he took
When on the gentle Severn's sedgy bank,
In single opposition, hand to hand,
He did confound the best part of an hour
In changing hardiment with great Glendower:
Three times they breathed and three times did they drink,
Upon agreement, of swift Severn's flood;
Who then, affrighted with their bloody looks,
Ran fearfully among the trembling reeds,
And hid his crisp head in the hollow bank,
Bloodstained with these valiant combatants.
Never did base and rotten policy
Colour her working with such deadly wounds;
Nor could the noble Mortimer
Receive so many, and all willingly:
Then let not him be slander'd with revolt.

**KING HENRY IV**

Thou dost belie him, Percy, thou dost belie him;
He never did encounter with Glendower:
I tell thee,
He durst as well have met the devil alone
As Owen Glendower for an enemy.
Art thou not ashamed? But, sirrah, henceforth
Let me not hear you speak of Mortimer:
Send me your prisoners with the speediest means,
Or you shall hear in such a kind from me
As will displease you. My Lord Northumberland,
We licence your departure with your son.
Send us your prisoners, or you will hear of it.

*Exeunt King Henry, Blunt, and train*

**HOTSPUR**

An if the devil come and roar for them,
I will not send them: I will after straight
And tell him so; for I will ease my heart,
Albeit I make a hazard of my head.

**NORTHUMBERLAND**

What, drunk with choler? stay and pause awhile:
Here comes your uncle.

*Re-enter WORCESTER*

**HOTSPUR**

Speak of Mortimer!
'Zounds, I will speak of him; and let my soul
Want mercy, if I do not join with him:
Yea, on his part I'll empty all these veins,
And shed my dear blood drop by drop in the dust,
But I will lift the down-trod Mortimer
As high in the air as this unthankful king,
As this ingrate and canker'd Bolingbroke.

**NORTHUMBERLAND**

Brother, the king hath made your nephew mad.

**EARL OF WORCESTER**

Who struck this heat up after I was gone?

**HOTSPUR**

He will, forsooth, have all my prisoners;
And when I urged the ransom once again
Of my wife's brother, then his cheek look'd pale,
And on my face he turn'd an eye of death,
Trembling even at the name of Mortimer.

**EARL OF WORCESTER**
I cannot blame him: was not he proclaim'd
By Richard that dead is the next of blood?
**NORTHUMBERLAND**
He was; I heard the proclamation:
And then it was when the unhappy king,
--Whose wrongs in us God pardon!--did set forth
Upon his Irish expedition;
From whence he intercepted did return
To be deposed and shortly murdered.
**EARL OF WORCESTER**
And for whose death we in the world's wide mouth
Live scandalized and foully spoken of.
**HOTSPUR**
But soft, I pray you; did King Richard then
Proclaim my brother Edmund Mortimer
Heir to the crown?
**NORTHUMBERLAND**
He did; myself did hear it.
**HOTSPUR**
Nay, then I cannot blame his cousin king,
That wished him on the barren mountains starve.
But shall it be that you, that set the crown
Upon the head of this forgetful man
And for his sake wear the detested blot
Of murderous subornation, shall it be,
That you a world of curses undergo,
Being the agents, or base second means,
The cords, the ladder, or the hangman rather?
O, pardon me that I descend so low,
To show the line and the predicament
Wherein you range under this subtle king;
Shall it for shame be spoken in these days,
Or fill up chronicles in time to come,
That men of your nobility and power
Did gage them both in an unjust behalf,
As both of you--God pardon it!--have done,
To put down Richard, that sweet lovely rose,
An plant this thorn, this canker, Bolingbroke?
And shall it in more shame be further spoken,
That you are fool'd, discarded and shook off
By him for whom these shames ye underwent?
No; yet time serves wherein you may redeem
Your banish'd honours and restore yourselves
Into the good thoughts of the world again,
Revenge the jeering and disdain'd contempt
Of this proud king, who studies day and night
To answer all the debt he owes to you
Even with the bloody payment of your deaths:
Therefore, I say--
**EARL OF WORCESTER**
Peace, cousin, say no more:
And now I will unclasp a secret book,
And to your quick-conceiving discontents
I'll read you matter deep and dangerous,
As full of peril and adventurous spirit
As to o'er-walk a current roaring loud
On the unsteadfast footing of a spear.
**HOTSPUR**
If he fall in, good night! or sink or swim:
Send danger from the east unto the west,
So honour cross it from the north to south,

And let them grapple: O, the blood more stirs
To rouse a lion than to start a hare!

**NORTHUMBERLAND**

Imagination of some great exploit
Drives him beyond the bounds of patience.

**HOTSPUR**

By heaven, methinks it were an easy leap,
To pluck bright honour from the pale-faced moon,
Or dive into the bottom of the deep,
Where fathom-line could never touch the ground,
And pluck up drowned honour by the locks;
So he that doth redeem her thence might wear
Without corrival, all her dignities:
But out upon this half-faced fellowship!

**EARL OF WORCESTER**

He apprehends a world of figures here,
But not the form of what he should attend.
Good cousin, give me audience for a while.

**HOTSPUR**

I cry you mercy.

**EARL OF WORCESTER**

Those same noble Scots
That are your prisoners,--

**HOTSPUR**

I'll keep them all;
By God, he shall not have a Scot of them;
No, if a Scot would save his soul, he shall not:
I'll keep them, by this hand.

**EARL OF WORCESTER**

You start away
And lend no ear unto my purposes.
Those prisoners you shall keep.

**HOTSPUR**

Nay, I will; that's flat:
He said he would not ransom Mortimer;
Forbad my tongue to speak of Mortimer;
But I will find him when he lies asleep,
And in his ear I'll holla 'Mortimer!'
Nay,
I'll have a starling shall be taught to speak
Nothing but 'Mortimer,' and give it him
To keep his anger still in motion.

**EARL OF WORCESTER**

Hear you, cousin; a word.

**HOTSPUR**

All studies here I solemnly defy,
Save how to gall and pinch this Bolingbroke:
And that same sword-and-buckler Prince of Wales,
But that I think his father loves him not
And would be glad he met with some mischance,
I would have him poison'd with a pot of ale.

**EARL OF WORCESTER**

Farewell, kinsman: I'll talk to you
When you are better temper'd to attend.

**NORTHUMBERLAND**

Why, what a wasp-stung and impatient fool
Art thou to break into this woman's mood,
Tying thine ear to no tongue but thine own!

**HOTSPUR**

Why, look you, I am whipp'd and scourged with rods,
Nettled and stung with pismires, when I hear
Of this vile politician, Bolingbroke.
In Richard's time,--what do you call the place?--

A plague upon it, it is in Gloucestershire;
'Twas where the madcap duke his uncle kept,
His uncle York; where I first bow'd my knee
Unto this king of smiles, this Bolingbroke,--
'Sblood!--
When you and he came back from Ravenspurgh.
**NORTHUMBERLAND**
At Berkley castle.
**HOTSPUR**
You say true:
Why, what a candy deal of courtesy
This fawning greyhound then did proffer me!
Look,'when his infant fortune came to age,'
And 'gentle Harry Percy,' and 'kind cousin;'
O, the devil take such cozeners! God forgive me!
Good uncle, tell your tale; I have done.
**EARL OF WORCESTER**
Nay, if you have not, to it again;
We will stay your leisure.
**HOTSPUR**
I have done, i' faith.
**EARL OF WORCESTER**
Then once more to your Scottish prisoners.
Deliver them up without their ransom straight,
And make the Douglas' son your only mean
For powers in Scotland; which, for divers reasons
Which I shall send you written, be assured,
Will easily be granted. You, my lord,
*To Northumberland*
Your son in Scotland being thus employ'd,
Shall secretly into the bosom creep
Of that same noble prelate, well beloved,
The archbishop.
**HOTSPUR**
Of York, is it not?
**EARL OF WORCESTER**
True; who bears hard
His brother's death at Bristol, the Lord Scroop.
I speak not this in estimation,
As what I think might be, but what I know
Is ruminated, plotted and set down,
And only stays but to behold the face
Of that occasion that shall bring it on.
**HOTSPUR**
I smell it: upon my life, it will do well.
**NORTHUMBERLAND**
Before the game is afoot, thou still let'st slip.
**HOTSPUR**
Why, it cannot choose but be a noble plot;
And then the power of Scotland and of York,
To join with Mortimer, ha?
**EARL OF WORCESTER**
And so they shall.
**HOTSPUR**
In faith, it is exceedingly well aim'd.
**EARL OF WORCESTER**
And 'tis no little reason bids us speed,
To save our heads by raising of a head;
For, bear ourselves as even as we can,
The king will always think him in our debt,
And think we think ourselves unsatisfied,
Till he hath found a time to pay us home:

And see already how he doth begin
To make us strangers to his looks of love.
**HOTSPUR**
He does, he does: we'll be revenged on him.
**EARL OF WORCESTER**
Cousin, farewell: no further go in this
Than I by letters shall direct your course.
When time is ripe, which will be suddenly,
I'll steal to Glendower and Lord Mortimer;
Where you and Douglas and our powers at once,
As I will fashion it, shall happily meet,
To bear our fortunes in our own strong arms,
Which now we hold at much uncertainty.
**NORTHUMBERLAND**
Farewell, good brother: we shall thrive, I trust.
**HOTSPUR**
Uncle, Adieu: O, let the hours be short
Till fields and blows and groans applaud our sport!
*Exeunt*

## ACT II

**SCENE I. Rochester. An inn yard.**

*Enter a Carrier with a lantern in his hand*

**First Carrier**

Heigh-ho! an it be not four by the day, I'll be
hanged: Charles' wain is over the new chimney, and
yet our horse not packed. What, ostler!

**Ostler**

[Within] Anon, anon.

**First Carrier**

I prithee, Tom, beat Cut's saddle, put a few flocks
in the point; poor jade, is wrung in the withers out
of all cess.

*Enter another Carrier*

**Second Carrier**

Peas and beans are as dank here as a dog, and that
is the next way to give poor jades the bots: this
house is turned upside down since Robin Ostler died.

**First Carrier**

Poor fellow, never joyed since the price of oats
rose; it was the death of him.

**Second Carrier**

I think this be the most villanous house in all
London road for fleas: I am stung like a tench.

**First Carrier**

Like a tench! by the mass, there is ne'er a king
christen could be better bit than I have been since
the first cock.

**Second Carrier**

Why, they will allow us ne'er a jordan, and then we
leak in your chimney; and your chamber-lie breeds
fleas like a loach.

**First Carrier**

What, ostler! come away and be hanged!

**Second Carrier**

I have a gammon of bacon and two razors of ginger,
to be delivered as far as Charing-cross.

**First Carrier**

God's body! the turkeys in my pannier are quite
starved. What, ostler! A plague on thee! hast thou
never an eye in thy head? canst not hear? An
'twere not as good deed as drink, to break the pate
on thee, I am a very villain. Come, and be hanged!
hast thou no faith in thee?

*Enter GADSHILL*

**GADSHILL**

Good morrow, carriers. What's o'clock?

**First Carrier**

I think it be two o'clock.

**GADSHILL**

I pray thee lend me thy lantern, to see my gelding
in the stable.

**First Carrier**

Nay, by God, soft; I know a trick worth two of that, i' faith.

**GADSHILL**

I pray thee, lend me thine.

**Second Carrier**

Ay, when? can'st tell? Lend me thy lantern, quoth
he? marry, I'll see thee hanged first.

**GADSHILL**

Sirrah carrier, what time do you mean to come to London?

**Second Carrier**

Time enough to go to bed with a candle, I warrant
thee. Come, neighbour Mugs, we'll call up the
gentleman: they will along with company, for they
have great charge.
*Exeunt carriers*
**GADSHILL**
What, ho! chamberlain!
**Chamberlain**
[Within] At hand, quoth pick-purse.
**GADSHILL**
That's even as fair as--at hand, quoth the
chamberlain; for thou variest no more from picking
of purses than giving direction doth from labouring;
thou layest the plot how.
*Enter Chamberlain*
**Chamberlain**
Good morrow, Master Gadshill. It holds current that
I told you yesternight: there's a franklin in the
wild of Kent hath brought three hundred marks with
him in gold: I heard him tell it to one of his
company last night at supper; a kind of auditor; one
that hath abundance of charge too, God knows what.
They are up already, and call for eggs and butter;
they will away presently.
**GADSHILL**
Sirrah, if they meet not with Saint Nicholas'
clerks, I'll give thee this neck.
**Chamberlain**
No, I'll none of it: I pray thee keep that for the
hangman; for I know thou worshippest St. Nicholas
as truly as a man of falsehood may.
**GADSHILL**
What talkest thou to me of the hangman? if I hang,
I'll make a fat pair of gallows; for if I hang, old
Sir John hangs with me, and thou knowest he is no
starveling. Tut! there are other Trojans that thou
dreamest not of, the which for sport sake are
content to do the profession some grace; that would,
if matters should be looked into, for their own
credit sake, make all whole. I am joined with no
foot-land rakers, no long-staff sixpenny strikers,
none of these mad mustachio purple-hued malt-worms;
but with nobility and tranquillity, burgomasters and
great oneyers, such as can hold in, such as will
strike sooner than speak, and speak sooner than
drink, and drink sooner than pray: and yet, zounds,
I lie; for they pray continually to their saint, the
commonwealth; or rather, not pray to her, but prey
on her, for they ride up and down on her and make
her their boots.
**Chamberlain**
What, the commonwealth their boots? will she hold
out water in foul way?
**GADSHILL**
She will, she will; justice hath liquored her. We
steal as in a castle, cocksure; we have the receipt
of fern-seed, we walk invisible.
**Chamberlain**
Nay, by my faith, I think you are more beholding to
the night than to fern-seed for your walking invisible.
**GADSHILL**
Give me thy hand: thou shalt have a share in our
purchase, as I am a true man.

**Chamberlain**
Nay, rather let me have it, as you are a false thief.
**GADSHILL**
Go to; 'homo' is a common name to all men. Bid the
ostler bring my gelding out of the stable. Farewell,
you muddy knave.
*Exeunt*
**SCENE II. The highway, near Gadshill.**
*Enter PRINCE HENRY and POINS*
**POINS**
Come, shelter, shelter: I have removed Falstaff's
horse, and he frets like a gummed velvet.
**PRINCE HENRY**
Stand close.
*Enter FALSTAFF*
**FALSTAFF**
Poins! Poins, and be hanged! Poins!
**PRINCE HENRY**
Peace, ye fat-kidneyed rascal! what a brawling dost
thou keep!
**FALSTAFF**
Where's Poins, Hal?
**PRINCE HENRY**
He is walked up to the top of the hill: I'll go seek him.
**FALSTAFF**
I am accursed to rob in that thief's company: the
rascal hath removed my horse, and tied him I know
not where. If I travel but four foot by the squier
further afoot, I shall break my wind. Well, I doubt
not but to die a fair death for all this, if I
'scape hanging for killing that rogue. I have
forsworn his company hourly any time this two and
twenty years, and yet I am bewitched with the
rogue's company. If the rascal hath not given me
medicines to make me love him, I'll be hanged; it
could not be else: I have drunk medicines. Poins!
Hal! a plague upon you both! Bardolph! Peto!
I'll starve ere I'll rob a foot further. An 'twere
not as good a deed as drink, to turn true man and to
leave these rogues, I am the veriest varlet that
ever chewed with a tooth. Eight yards of uneven
ground is threescore and ten miles afoot with me;
and the stony-hearted villains know it well enough:
a plague upon it when thieves cannot be true one to another!
*They whistle*
Whew! A plague upon you all! Give me my horse, you
rogues; give me my horse, and be hanged!
**PRINCE HENRY**
Peace, ye fat-guts! lie down; lay thine ear close
to the ground and list if thou canst hear the tread
of travellers.
**FALSTAFF**
Have you any levers to lift me up again, being down?
'Sblood, I'll not bear mine own flesh so far afoot
again for all the coin in thy father's exchequer.
What a plague mean ye to colt me thus?
**PRINCE HENRY**
Thou liest; thou art not colted, thou art uncolted.
**FALSTAFF**
I prithee, good Prince Hal, help me to my horse,
good king's son.
**PRINCE HENRY**
Out, ye rogue! shall I be your ostler?

**FALSTAFF**
Go, hang thyself in thine own heir-apparent garters! If I be ta'en, I'll peach for this. An I have not ballads made on you all and sung to filthy tunes, let a cup of sack be my poison: when a jest is so forward, and afoot too! I hate it.
*Enter GADSHILL, BARDOLPH and PETO*
**GADSHILL**
Stand.
**FALSTAFF**
So I do, against my will.
**POINS**
O, 'tis our setter: I know his voice. Bardolph, what news?
**BARDOLPH**
Case ye, case ye; on with your vizards: there 's money of the king's coming down the hill; 'tis going to the king's exchequer.
**FALSTAFF**
You lie, ye rogue; 'tis going to the king's tavern.
**GADSHILL**
There's enough to make us all.
**FALSTAFF**
To be hanged.
**PRINCE HENRY**
Sirs, you four shall front them in the narrow lane; Ned Poins and I will walk lower: if they 'scape from your encounter, then they light on us.
**PETO**
How many be there of them?
**GADSHILL**
Some eight or ten.
**FALSTAFF**
'Zounds, will they not rob us?
**PRINCE HENRY**
What, a coward, Sir John Paunch?
**FALSTAFF**
Indeed, I am not John of Gaunt, your grandfather; but yet no coward, Hal.
**PRINCE HENRY**
Well, we leave that to the proof.
**POINS**
Sirrah Jack, thy horse stands behind the hedge: when thou needest him, there thou shalt find him. Farewell, and stand fast.
**FALSTAFF**
Now cannot I strike him, if I should be hanged.
**PRINCE HENRY**
Ned, where are our disguises?
**POINS**
Here, hard by: stand close.
*Exeunt PRINCE HENRY and POINS*
**FALSTAFF**
Now, my masters, happy man be his dole, say I: every man to his business.
*Enter the Travellers*
**First Traveller**
Come, neighbour: the boy shall lead our horses down the hill; we'll walk afoot awhile, and ease our legs.
**Thieves**
Stand!
**Travellers**
Jesus bless us!

**FALSTAFF**
Strike; down with them; cut the villains' throats:
ah! whoreson caterpillars! bacon-fed knaves! they
hate us youth: down with them: fleece them.
**Travellers**
O, we are undone, both we and ours for ever!
**FALSTAFF**
Hang ye, gorbellied knaves, are ye undone? No, ye
fat chuffs: I would your store were here! On,
bacons, on! What, ye knaves! young men must live.
You are Grand-jurors, are ye? we'll jure ye, 'faith.
*Here they rob them and bind them. Exeunt*
*Re-enter PRINCE HENRY and POINS*
**PRINCE HENRY**
The thieves have bound the true men. Now could thou
and I rob the thieves and go merrily to London, it
would be argument for a week, laughter for a month
and a good jest for ever.
**POINS**
Stand close; I hear them coming.
*Enter the Thieves again*
**FALSTAFF**
Come, my masters, let us share, and then to horse
before day. An the Prince and Poins be not two
arrant cowards, there's no equity stirring: there's
no more valour in that Poins than in a wild-duck.
**PRINCE HENRY**
Your money!
**POINS**
Villains!
*As they are sharing, the Prince and Poins set upon them; they all run away; and Falstaff, after a blow or two, runs away too, leaving the booty behind them*
**PRINCE HENRY**
Got with much ease. Now merrily to horse:
The thieves are all scatter'd and possess'd with fear
So strongly that they dare not meet each other;
Each takes his fellow for an officer.
Away, good Ned. Falstaff sweats to death,
And lards the lean earth as he walks along:
Were 't not for laughing, I should pity him.
**POINS**
How the rogue roar'd!
*Exeunt*
**SCENE III. Warkworth castle**
*Enter HOTSPUR, solus, reading a letter*
**HOTSPUR**
'But for mine own part, my lord, I could be well
contented to be there, in respect of the love I bear
your house.' He could be contented: why is he not,
then? In respect of the love he bears our house:
he shows in this, he loves his own barn better than
he loves our house. Let me see some more. 'The
purpose you undertake is dangerous;'--why, that's
certain: 'tis dangerous to take a cold, to sleep, to
drink; but I tell you, my lord fool, out of this
nettle, danger, we pluck this flower, safety. 'The
purpose you undertake is dangerous; the friends you
have named uncertain; the time itself unsorted; and
your whole plot too light for the counterpoise of so
great an opposition.' Say you so, say you so? I say
unto you again, you are a shallow cowardly hind, and
you lie. What a lack-brain is this! By the Lord,
our plot is a good plot as ever was laid; our

friends true and constant: a good plot, good
friends, and full of expectation; an excellent plot,
very good friends. What a frosty-spirited rogue is
this! Why, my lord of York commends the plot and the
general course of action. 'Zounds, an I were now by
this rascal, I could brain him with his lady's fan.
Is there not my father, my uncle and myself? lord
Edmund Mortimer, My lord of York and Owen Glendower?
is there not besides the Douglas? have I not all
their letters to meet me in arms by the ninth of the
next month? and are they not some of them set
forward already? What a pagan rascal is this! an
infidel! Ha! you shall see now in very sincerity
of fear and cold heart, will he to the king and lay
open all our proceedings. O, I could divide myself
and go to buffets, for moving such a dish of
skim milk with so honourable an action! Hang him!
let him tell the king: we are prepared. I will set
forward to-night.
*Enter LADY PERCY*
How now, Kate! I must leave you within these two hours.
**LADY PERCY**
O, my good lord, why are you thus alone?
For what offence have I this fortnight been
A banish'd woman from my Harry's bed?
Tell me, sweet lord, what is't that takes from thee
Thy stomach, pleasure and thy golden sleep?
Why dost thou bend thine eyes upon the earth,
And start so often when thou sit'st alone?
Why hast thou lost the fresh blood in thy cheeks;
And given my treasures and my rights of thee
To thick-eyed musing and cursed melancholy?
In thy faint slumbers I by thee have watch'd,
And heard thee murmur tales of iron wars;
Speak terms of manage to thy bounding steed;
Cry 'Courage! to the field!' And thou hast talk'd
Of sallies and retires, of trenches, tents,
Of palisadoes, frontiers, parapets,
Of basilisks, of cannon, culverin,
Of prisoners' ransom and of soldiers slain,
And all the currents of a heady fight.
Thy spirit within thee hath been so at war
And thus hath so bestirr'd thee in thy sleep,
That beads of sweat have stood upon thy brow
Like bubbles in a late-disturbed stream;
And in thy face strange motions have appear'd,
Such as we see when men restrain their breath
On some great sudden hest. O, what portents are these?
Some heavy business hath my lord in hand,
And I must know it, else he loves me not.
**HOTSPUR**
What, ho!
*Enter Servant*
Is Gilliams with the packet gone?
**Servant**
He is, my lord, an hour ago.
**HOTSPUR**
Hath Butler brought those horses from the sheriff?
**Servant**
One horse, my lord, he brought even now.
**HOTSPUR**
What horse? a roan, a crop-ear, is it not?
**Servant**

It is, my lord.
**HOTSPUR**
That roan shall by my throne.
Well, I will back him straight: O esperance!
Bid Butler lead him forth into the park.
*Exit Servant*
**LADY PERCY**
But hear you, my lord.
**HOTSPUR**
What say'st thou, my lady?
**LADY PERCY**
What is it carries you away?
**HOTSPUR**
Why, my horse, my love, my horse.
**LADY PERCY**
Out, you mad-headed ape!
A weasel hath not such a deal of spleen
As you are toss'd with. In faith,
I'll know your business, Harry, that I will.
I fear my brother Mortimer doth stir
About his title, and hath sent for you
To line his enterprise: but if you go,--
**HOTSPUR**
So far afoot, I shall be weary, love.
**LADY PERCY**
Come, come, you paraquito, answer me
Directly unto this question that I ask:
In faith, I'll break thy little finger, Harry,
An if thou wilt not tell me all things true.
**HOTSPUR**
Away,
Away, you trifler! Love! I love thee not,
I care not for thee, Kate: this is no world
To play with mammets and to tilt with lips:
We must have bloody noses and crack'd crowns,
And pass them current too. God's me, my horse!
What say'st thou, Kate? what would'st thou
have with me?
**LADY PERCY**
Do you not love me? do you not, indeed?
Well, do not then; for since you love me not,
I will not love myself. Do you not love me?
Nay, tell me if you speak in jest or no.
**HOTSPUR**
Come, wilt thou see me ride?
And when I am on horseback, I will swear
I love thee infinitely. But hark you, Kate;
I must not have you henceforth question me
Whither I go, nor reason whereabout:
Whither I must, I must; and, to conclude,
This evening must I leave you, gentle Kate.
I know you wise, but yet no farther wise
Than Harry Percy's wife: constant you are,
But yet a woman: and for secrecy,
No lady closer; for I well believe
Thou wilt not utter what thou dost not know;
And so far will I trust thee, gentle Kate.
**LADY PERCY**
How! so far?
**HOTSPUR**
Not an inch further. But hark you, Kate:
Whither I go, thither shall you go too;

To-day will I set forth, to-morrow you.
Will this content you, Kate?
**LADY PERCY**
It must of force.
*Exeunt*
**SCENE IV. The Boar's-Head Tavern, Eastcheap.**
*Enter PRINCE HENRY and POINS*
**PRINCE HENRY**
Ned, prithee, come out of that fat room, and lend me
thy hand to laugh a little.
**POINS**
Where hast been, Hal?
**PRINCE HENRY**
With three or four loggerheads amongst three or four
score hogsheads. I have sounded the very
base-string of humility. Sirrah, I am sworn brother
to a leash of drawers; and can call them all by
their christen names, as Tom, Dick, and Francis.
They take it already upon their salvation, that
though I be but the prince of Wales, yet I am king
of courtesy; and tell me flatly I am no proud Jack,
like Falstaff, but a Corinthian, a lad of mettle, a
good boy, by the Lord, so they call me, and when I
am king of England, I shall command all the good
lads in Eastcheap. They call drinking deep, dyeing
scarlet; and when you breathe in your watering, they
cry 'hem!' and bid you play it off. To conclude, I
am so good a proficient in one quarter of an hour,
that I can drink with any tinker in his own language
during my life. I tell thee, Ned, thou hast lost
much honour, that thou wert not with me in this sweet
action. But, sweet Ned,--to sweeten which name of
Ned, I give thee this pennyworth of sugar, clapped
even now into my hand by an under-skinker, one that
never spake other English in his life than 'Eight
shillings and sixpence' and 'You are welcome,' with
this shrill addition, 'Anon, anon, sir! Score a pint
of bastard in the Half-Moon,' or so. But, Ned, to
drive away the time till Falstaff come, I prithee,
do thou stand in some by-room, while I question my
puny drawer to what end he gave me the sugar; and do
thou never leave calling 'Francis,' that his tale
to me may be nothing but 'Anon.' Step aside, and
I'll show thee a precedent.
**POINS**
Francis!
**PRINCE HENRY**
Thou art perfect.
**POINS**
Francis!
*Exit POINS*
*Enter FRANCIS*
**FRANCIS**
Anon, anon, sir. Look down into the Pomgarnet, Ralph.
**PRINCE HENRY**
Come hither, Francis.
**FRANCIS**
My lord?
**PRINCE HENRY**
How long hast thou to serve, Francis?
**FRANCIS**
Forsooth, five years, and as much as to--
**POINS**

[Within] Francis!
**FRANCIS**
Anon, anon, sir.
**PRINCE HENRY**
Five year! by'r lady, a long lease for the clinking
of pewter. But, Francis, darest thou be so valiant
as to play the coward with thy indenture and show it
a fair pair of heels and run from it?
**FRANCIS**
O Lord, sir, I'll be sworn upon all the books in
England, I could find in my heart.
**POINS**
[Within] Francis!
**FRANCIS**
Anon, sir.
**PRINCE HENRY**
How old art thou, Francis?
**FRANCIS**
Let me see--about Michaelmas next I shall be--
**POINS**
[Within] Francis!
**FRANCIS**
Anon, sir. Pray stay a little, my lord.
**PRINCE HENRY**
Nay, but hark you, Francis: for the sugar thou
gavest me,'twas a pennyworth, wast't not?
**FRANCIS**
O Lord, I would it had been two!
**PRINCE HENRY**
I will give thee for it a thousand pound: ask me
when thou wilt, and thou shalt have it.
**POINS**
[Within] Francis!
**FRANCIS**
Anon, anon.
**PRINCE HENRY**
Anon, Francis? No, Francis; but to-morrow, Francis;
or, Francis, o' Thursday; or indeed, Francis, when
thou wilt. But, Francis!
**FRANCIS**
My lord?
**PRINCE HENRY**
Wilt thou rob this leathern jerkin, crystal-button,
not-pated, agate-ring, puke-stocking, caddis-garter,
smooth-tongue, Spanish-pouch,--
**FRANCIS**
O Lord, sir, who do you mean?
**PRINCE HENRY**
Why, then, your brown bastard is your only drink;
for look you, Francis, your white canvas doublet
will sully: in Barbary, sir, it cannot come to so much.
**FRANCIS**
What, sir?
**POINS**
[Within] Francis!
**PRINCE HENRY**
Away, you rogue! dost thou not hear them call?
*Here they both call him; the drawer stands amazed, not knowing which way to go*
*Enter Vintner*
**Vintner**
What, standest thou still, and hearest such a
calling? Look to the guests within.
*Exit Francis*

My lord, old Sir John, with half-a-dozen more, are
at the door: shall I let them in?
**PRINCE HENRY**
Let them alone awhile, and then open the door.
*Exit Vintner*
Poins!
*Re-enter POINS*
**POINS**
Anon, anon, sir.
**PRINCE HENRY**
Sirrah, Falstaff and the rest of the thieves are at
the door: shall we be merry?
**POINS**
As merry as crickets, my lad. But hark ye; what
cunning match have you made with this jest of the
drawer? come, what's the issue?
**PRINCE HENRY**
I am now of all humours that have showed themselves
humours since the old days of goodman Adam to the
pupil age of this present twelve o'clock at midnight.
*Re-enter FRANCIS*
What's o'clock, Francis?
**FRANCIS**
Anon, anon, sir.
*Exit*
**PRINCE HENRY**
That ever this fellow should have fewer words than a
parrot, and yet the son of a woman! His industry is
upstairs and downstairs; his eloquence the parcel of
a reckoning. I am not yet of Percy's mind, the
Hotspur of the north; he that kills me some six or
seven dozen of Scots at a breakfast, washes his
hands, and says to his wife 'Fie upon this quiet
life! I want work.' 'O my sweet Harry,' says she,
'how many hast thou killed to-day?' 'Give my roan
horse a drench,' says he; and answers 'Some
fourteen,' an hour after; 'a trifle, a trifle.' I
prithee, call in Falstaff: I'll play Percy, and
that damned brawn shall play Dame Mortimer his
wife. 'Rivo!' says the drunkard. Call in ribs, call in tallow.
*Enter FALSTAFF, GADSHILL, BARDOLPH, and PETO; FRANCIS following with wine*
**POINS**
Welcome, Jack: where hast thou been?
**FALSTAFF**
A plague of all cowards, I say, and a vengeance too!
marry, and amen! Give me a cup of sack, boy. Ere I
lead this life long, I'll sew nether stocks and mend
them and foot them too. A plague of all cowards!
Give me a cup of sack, rogue. Is there no virtue extant?
*He drinks*
**PRINCE HENRY**
Didst thou never see Titan kiss a dish of butter?
pitiful-hearted Titan, that melted at the sweet tale
of the sun's! if thou didst, then behold that compound.
**FALSTAFF**
You rogue, here's lime in this sack too: there is
nothing but roguery to be found in villanous man:
yet a coward is worse than a cup of sack with lime
in it. A villanous coward! Go thy ways, old Jack;
die when thou wilt, if manhood, good manhood, be
not forgot upon the face of the earth, then am I a
shotten herring. There live not three good men
unhanged in England; and one of them is fat and

grows old: God help the while! a bad world, I say.
I would I were a weaver; I could sing psalms or any
thing. A plague of all cowards, I say still.

**PRINCE HENRY**

How now, wool-sack! what mutter you?

**FALSTAFF**

A king's son! If I do not beat thee out of thy
kingdom with a dagger of lath, and drive all thy
subjects afore thee like a flock of wild-geese,
I'll never wear hair on my face more. You Prince of Wales!

**PRINCE HENRY**

Why, you whoreson round man, what's the matter?

**FALSTAFF**

Are not you a coward? answer me to that: and Poins there?

**POINS**

'Zounds, ye fat paunch, an ye call me coward, by the
Lord, I'll stab thee.

**FALSTAFF**

I call thee coward! I'll see thee damned ere I call
thee coward: but I would give a thousand pound I
could run as fast as thou canst. You are straight
enough in the shoulders, you care not who sees your
back: call you that backing of your friends? A
plague upon such backing! give me them that will
face me. Give me a cup of sack: I am a rogue, if I
drunk to-day.

**PRINCE HENRY**

O villain! thy lips are scarce wiped since thou
drunkest last.

**FALSTAFF**

All's one for that.

*He drinks*

A plague of all cowards, still say I.

**PRINCE HENRY**

What's the matter?

**FALSTAFF**

What's the matter! there be four of us here have
ta'en a thousand pound this day morning.

**PRINCE HENRY**

Where is it, Jack? where is it?

**FALSTAFF**

Where is it! taken from us it is: a hundred upon
poor four of us.

**PRINCE HENRY**

What, a hundred, man?

**FALSTAFF**

I am a rogue, if I were not at half-sword with a
dozen of them two hours together. I have 'scaped by
miracle. I am eight times thrust through the
doublet, four through the hose; my buckler cut
through and through; my sword hacked like a
hand-saw--ecce signum! I never dealt better since
I was a man: all would not do. A plague of all
cowards! Let them speak: if they speak more or
less than truth, they are villains and the sons of darkness.

**PRINCE HENRY**

Speak, sirs; how was it?

**GADSHILL**

We four set upon some dozen--

**FALSTAFF**

Sixteen at least, my lord.

**GADSHILL**

And bound them.

**PETO**
No, no, they were not bound.
**FALSTAFF**
You rogue, they were bound, every man of them; or I
am a Jew else, an Ebrew Jew.
**GADSHILL**
As we were sharing, some six or seven fresh men set upon us--
**FALSTAFF**
And unbound the rest, and then come in the other.
**PRINCE HENRY**
What, fought you with them all?
**FALSTAFF**
All! I know not what you call all; but if I fought
not with fifty of them, I am a bunch of radish: if
there were not two or three and fifty upon poor old
Jack, then am I no two-legged creature.
**PRINCE HENRY**
Pray God you have not murdered some of them.
**FALSTAFF**
Nay, that's past praying for: I have peppered two
of them; two I am sure I have paid, two rogues
in buckram suits. I tell thee what, Hal, if I tell
thee a lie, spit in my face, call me horse. Thou
knowest my old ward; here I lay and thus I bore my
point. Four rogues in buckram let drive at me--
**PRINCE HENRY**
What, four? thou saidst but two even now.
**FALSTAFF**
Four, Hal; I told thee four.
**POINS**
Ay, ay, he said four.
**FALSTAFF**
These four came all a-front, and mainly thrust at
me. I made me no more ado but took all their seven
points in my target, thus.
**PRINCE HENRY**
Seven? why, there were but four even now.
**FALSTAFF**
In buckram?
**POINS**
Ay, four, in buckram suits.
**FALSTAFF**
Seven, by these hilts, or I am a villain else.
**PRINCE HENRY**
Prithee, let him alone; we shall have more anon.
**FALSTAFF**
Dost thou hear me, Hal?
**PRINCE HENRY**
Ay, and mark thee too, Jack.
**FALSTAFF**
Do so, for it is worth the listening to. These nine
in buckram that I told thee of--
**PRINCE HENRY**
So, two more already.
**FALSTAFF**
Their points being broken,--
**POINS**
Down fell their hose.
**FALSTAFF**
Began to give me ground: but I followed me close,
came in foot and hand; and with a thought seven of
the eleven I paid.
**PRINCE HENRY**

O monstrous! eleven buckram men grown out of two!
**FALSTAFF**
But, as the devil would have it, three misbegotten knaves in Kendal green came at my back and let drive at me; for it was so dark, Hal, that thou couldst not see thy hand.
**PRINCE HENRY**
These lies are like their father that begets them; gross as a mountain, open, palpable. Why, thou clay-brained guts, thou knotty-pated fool, thou whoreson, obscene, grease tallow-catch,--
**FALSTAFF**
What, art thou mad? art thou mad? is not the truth the truth?
**PRINCE HENRY**
Why, how couldst thou know these men in Kendal green, when it was so dark thou couldst not see thy hand? come, tell us your reason: what sayest thou to this?
**POINS**
Come, your reason, Jack, your reason.
**FALSTAFF**
What, upon compulsion? 'Zounds, an I were at the strappado, or all the racks in the world, I would not tell you on compulsion. Give you a reason on compulsion! If reasons were as plentiful as blackberries, I would give no man a reason upon compulsion, I.
**PRINCE HENRY**
I'll be no longer guilty of this sin; this sanguine coward, this bed-presser, this horseback-breaker, this huge hill of flesh,--
**FALSTAFF**
'Sblood, you starveling, you elf-skin, you dried neat's tongue, you bull's pizzle, you stock-fish! O for breath to utter what is like thee! you tailor's-yard, you sheath, you bowcase; you vile standing-tuck,--
**PRINCE HENRY**
Well, breathe awhile, and then to it again: and when thou hast tired thyself in base comparisons, hear me speak but this.
**POINS**
Mark, Jack.
**PRINCE HENRY**
We two saw you four set on four and bound them, and were masters of their wealth. Mark now, how a plain tale shall put you down. Then did we two set on you four; and, with a word, out-faced you from your prize, and have it; yea, and can show it you here in the house: and, Falstaff, you carried your guts away as nimbly, with as quick dexterity, and roared for mercy and still run and roared, as ever I heard bull-calf. What a slave art thou, to hack thy sword as thou hast done, and then say it was in fight! What trick, what device, what starting-hole, canst thou now find out to hide thee from this open and apparent shame?
**POINS**
Come, let's hear, Jack; what trick hast thou now?
**FALSTAFF**
By the Lord, I knew ye as well as he that made ye. Why, hear you, my masters: was it for me to kill the heir-apparent? should I turn upon the true prince?

why, thou knowest I am as valiant as Hercules: but
beware instinct; the lion will not touch the true
prince. Instinct is a great matter; I was now a
coward on instinct. I shall think the better of
myself and thee during my life; I for a valiant
lion, and thou for a true prince. But, by the Lord,
lads, I am glad you have the money. Hostess, clap
to the doors: watch to-night, pray to-morrow.
Gallants, lads, boys, hearts of gold, all the titles
of good fellowship come to you! What, shall we be
merry? shall we have a play extempore?

**PRINCE HENRY**

Content; and the argument shall be thy running away.

**FALSTAFF**

Ah, no more of that, Hal, an thou lovest me!

*Enter Hostess*

**Hostess**

O Jesu, my lord the prince!

**PRINCE HENRY**

How now, my lady the hostess! what sayest thou to
me?

**Hostess**

Marry, my lord, there is a nobleman of the court at
door would speak with you: he says he comes from
your father.

**PRINCE HENRY**

Give him as much as will make him a royal man, and
send him back again to my mother.

**FALSTAFF**

What manner of man is he?

**Hostess**

An old man.

**FALSTAFF**

What doth gravity out of his bed at midnight? Shall
I give him his answer?

**PRINCE HENRY**

Prithee, do, Jack.

**FALSTAFF**

'Faith, and I'll send him packing.

*Exit FALSTAFF*

**PRINCE HENRY**

Now, sirs: by'r lady, you fought fair; so did you,
Peto; so did you, Bardolph: you are lions too, you
ran away upon instinct, you will not touch the true
prince; no, fie!

**BARDOLPH**

'Faith, I ran when I saw others run.

**PRINCE HENRY**

'Faith, tell me now in earnest, how came Falstaff's
sword so hacked?

**PETO**

Why, he hacked it with his dagger, and said he would
swear truth out of England but he would make you
believe it was done in fight, and persuaded us to do the like.

**BARDOLPH**

Yea, and to tickle our noses with spear-grass to
make them bleed, and then to beslubber our garments
with it and swear it was the blood of true men. I
did that I did not this seven year before, I blushed
to hear his monstrous devices.

**PRINCE HENRY**

O villain, thou stolest a cup of sack eighteen years
ago, and wert taken with the manner, and ever since

thou hast blushed extempore. Thou hadst fire and
sword on thy side, and yet thou rannest away: what
instinct hadst thou for it?
**BARDOLPH**
My lord, do you see these meteors? do you behold
these exhalations?
**PRINCE HENRY**
I do.
**BARDOLPH**
What think you they portend?
**PRINCE HENRY**
Hot livers and cold purses.
**BARDOLPH**
Choler, my lord, if rightly taken.
**PRINCE HENRY**
No, if rightly taken, halter.
*Re-enter FALSTAFF*
Here comes lean Jack, here comes bare-bone.
How now, my sweet creature of bombast!
How long is't ago, Jack, since thou sawest thine own knee?
**FALSTAFF**
My own knee! when I was about thy years, Hal, I was
not an eagle's talon in the waist; I could have
crept into any alderman's thumb-ring: a plague of
sighing and grief! it blows a man up like a
bladder. There's villanous news abroad: here was
Sir John Bracy from your father; you must to the
court in the morning. That same mad fellow of the
north, Percy, and he of Wales, that gave Amamon the
bastinado and made Lucifer cuckold and swore the
devil his true liegeman upon the cross of a Welsh
hook--what a plague call you him?
**POINS**
O, Glendower.
**FALSTAFF**
Owen, Owen, the same; and his son-in-law Mortimer,
and old Northumberland, and that sprightly Scot of
Scots, Douglas, that runs o' horseback up a hill
perpendicular,--
**PRINCE HENRY**
He that rides at high speed and with his pistol
kills a sparrow flying.
**FALSTAFF**
You have hit it.
**PRINCE HENRY**
So did he never the sparrow.
**FALSTAFF**
Well, that rascal hath good mettle in him; he will not run.
**PRINCE HENRY**
Why, what a rascal art thou then, to praise him so
for running!
**FALSTAFF**
O' horseback, ye cuckoo; but afoot he will not budge a foot.
**PRINCE HENRY**
Yes, Jack, upon instinct.
**FALSTAFF**
I grant ye, upon instinct. Well, he is there too,
and one Mordake, and a thousand blue-caps more:
Worcester is stolen away to-night; thy father's
beard is turned white with the news: you may buy
land now as cheap as stinking mackerel.
**PRINCE HENRY**

Why, then, it is like, if there come a hot June and
this civil buffeting hold, we shall buy maidenheads
as they buy hob-nails, by the hundreds.

**FALSTAFF**

By the mass, lad, thou sayest true; it is like we
shall have good trading that way. But tell me, Hal,
art not thou horrible afeard? thou being
heir-apparent, could the world pick thee out three
such enemies again as that fiend Douglas, that
spirit Percy, and that devil Glendower? Art thou
not horribly afraid? doth not thy blood thrill at
it?

**PRINCE HENRY**

Not a whit, i' faith; I lack some of thy instinct.

**FALSTAFF**

Well, thou wert be horribly chid tomorrow when thou
comest to thy father: if thou love me, practise an answer.

**PRINCE HENRY**

Do thou stand for my father, and examine me upon the
particulars of my life.

**FALSTAFF**

Shall I? content: this chair shall be my state,
this dagger my sceptre, and this cushion my crown.

**PRINCE HENRY**

Thy state is taken for a joined-stool, thy golden
sceptre for a leaden dagger, and thy precious rich
crown for a pitiful bald crown!

**FALSTAFF**

Well, an the fire of grace be not quite out of thee,
now shalt thou be moved. Give me a cup of sack to
make my eyes look red, that it may be thought I have
wept; for I must speak in passion, and I will do it
in King Cambyses' vein.

**PRINCE HENRY**

Well, here is my leg.

**FALSTAFF**

And here is my speech. Stand aside, nobility.

**Hostess**

O Jesu, this is excellent sport, i' faith!

**FALSTAFF**

Weep not, sweet queen; for trickling tears are vain.

**Hostess**

O, the father, how he holds his countenance!

**FALSTAFF**

For God's sake, lords, convey my tristful queen;
For tears do stop the flood-gates of her eyes.

**Hostess**

O Jesu, he doth it as like one of these harlotry
players as ever I see!

**FALSTAFF**

Peace, good pint-pot; peace, good tickle-brain.
Harry, I do not only marvel where thou spendest thy
time, but also how thou art accompanied: for though
the camomile, the more it is trodden on the faster
it grows, yet youth, the more it is wasted the
sooner it wears. That thou art my son, I have
partly thy mother's word, partly my own opinion,
but chiefly a villanous trick of thine eye and a
foolish-hanging of thy nether lip, that doth warrant
me. If then thou be son to me, here lies the point;
why, being son to me, art thou so pointed at? Shall
the blessed sun of heaven prove a micher and eat
blackberries? a question not to be asked. Shall

the sun of England prove a thief and take purses? a
question to be asked. There is a thing, Harry,
which thou hast often heard of and it is known to
many in our land by the name of pitch: this pitch,
as ancient writers do report, doth defile; so doth
the company thou keepest: for, Harry, now I do not
speak to thee in drink but in tears, not in
pleasure but in passion, not in words only, but in
woes also: and yet there is a virtuous man whom I
have often noted in thy company, but I know not his name.

**PRINCE HENRY**

What manner of man, an it like your majesty?

**FALSTAFF**

A goodly portly man, i' faith, and a corpulent; of a
cheerful look, a pleasing eye and a most noble
carriage; and, as I think, his age some fifty, or,
by'r lady, inclining to three score; and now I
remember me, his name is Falstaff: if that man
should be lewdly given, he deceiveth me; for, Harry,
I see virtue in his looks. If then the tree may be
known by the fruit, as the fruit by the tree, then,
peremptorily I speak it, there is virtue in that
Falstaff: him keep with, the rest banish. And tell
me now, thou naughty varlet, tell me, where hast
thou been this month?

**PRINCE HENRY**

Dost thou speak like a king? Do thou stand for me,
and I'll play my father.

**FALSTAFF**

Depose me? if thou dost it half so gravely, so
majestically, both in word and matter, hang me up by
the heels for a rabbit-sucker or a poulter's hare.

**PRINCE HENRY**

Well, here I am set.

**FALSTAFF**

And here I stand: judge, my masters.

**PRINCE HENRY**

Now, Harry, whence come you?

**FALSTAFF**

My noble lord, from Eastcheap.

**PRINCE HENRY**

The complaints I hear of thee are grievous.

**FALSTAFF**

'Sblood, my lord, they are false: nay, I'll tickle
ye for a young prince, i' faith.

**PRINCE HENRY**

Swearest thou, ungracious boy? henceforth ne'er look
on me. Thou art violently carried away from grace:
there is a devil haunts thee in the likeness of an
old fat man; a tun of man is thy companion. Why
dost thou converse with that trunk of humours, that
bolting-hutch of beastliness, that swollen parcel
of dropsies, that huge bombard of sack, that stuffed
cloak-bag of guts, that roasted Manningtree ox with
the pudding in his belly, that reverend vice, that
grey iniquity, that father ruffian, that vanity in
years? Wherein is he good, but to taste sack and
drink it? wherein neat and cleanly, but to carve a
capon and eat it? wherein cunning, but in craft?
wherein crafty, but in villany? wherein villanous,
but in all things? wherein worthy, but in nothing?

**FALSTAFF**

I would your grace would take me with you: whom
means your grace?
**PRINCE HENRY**
That villanous abominable misleader of youth,
Falstaff, that old white-bearded Satan.
**FALSTAFF**
My lord, the man I know.
**PRINCE HENRY**
I know thou dost.
**FALSTAFF**
But to say I know more harm in him than in myself,
were to say more than I know. That he is old, the
more the pity, his white hairs do witness it; but
that he is, saving your reverence, a whoremaster,
that I utterly deny. If sack and sugar be a fault,
God help the wicked! if to be old and merry be a
sin, then many an old host that I know is damned: if
to be fat be to be hated, then Pharaoh's lean kine
are to be loved. No, my good lord; banish Peto,
banish Bardolph, banish Poins: but for sweet Jack
Falstaff, kind Jack Falstaff, true Jack Falstaff,
valiant Jack Falstaff, and therefore more valiant,
being, as he is, old Jack Falstaff, banish not him
thy Harry's company, banish not him thy Harry's
company: banish plump Jack, and banish all the world.
**PRINCE HENRY**
I do, I will.
*A knocking heard*
*Exeunt Hostess, FRANCIS, and BARDOLPH*
*Re-enter BARDOLPH, running*
**BARDOLPH**
O, my lord, my lord! the sheriff with a most
monstrous watch is at the door.
**FALSTAFF**
Out, ye rogue! Play out the play: I have much to
say in the behalf of that Falstaff.
*Re-enter the Hostess*
**Hostess**
O Jesu, my lord, my lord!
**PRINCE HENRY**
Heigh, heigh! the devil rides upon a fiddlestick:
what's the matter?
**Hostess**
The sheriff and all the watch are at the door: they
are come to search the house. Shall I let them in?
**FALSTAFF**
Dost thou hear, Hal? never call a true piece of
gold a counterfeit: thou art essentially mad,
without seeming so.
**PRINCE HENRY**
And thou a natural coward, without instinct.
**FALSTAFF**
I deny your major: if you will deny the sheriff,
so; if not, let him enter: if I become not a cart
as well as another man, a plague on my bringing up!
I hope I shall as soon be strangled with a halter as another.
**PRINCE HENRY**
Go, hide thee behind the arras: the rest walk up
above. Now, my masters, for a true face and good
conscience.
**FALSTAFF**
Both which I have had: but their date is out, and
therefore I'll hide me.

**PRINCE HENRY**
Call in the sheriff.
*Exeunt all except PRINCE HENRY and PETO*
*Enter Sheriff and the Carrier*
Now, master sheriff, what is your will with me?
**Sheriff**
First, pardon me, my lord. A hue and cry
Hath follow'd certain men unto this house.
**PRINCE HENRY**
What men?
**Sheriff**
One of them is well known, my gracious lord,
A gross fat man.
**Carrier**
As fat as butter.
**PRINCE HENRY**
The man, I do assure you, is not here;
For I myself at this time have employ'd him.
And, sheriff, I will engage my word to thee
That I will, by to-morrow dinner-time,
Send him to answer thee, or any man,
For any thing he shall be charged withal:
And so let me entreat you leave the house.
**Sheriff**
I will, my lord. There are two gentlemen
Have in this robbery lost three hundred marks.
**PRINCE HENRY**
It may be so: if he have robb'd these men,
He shall be answerable; and so farewell.
**Sheriff**
Good night, my noble lord.
**PRINCE HENRY**
I think it is good morrow, is it not?
**Sheriff**
Indeed, my lord, I think it be two o'clock.
*Exeunt Sheriff and Carrier*
**PRINCE HENRY**
This oily rascal is known as well as Paul's. Go,
call him forth.
**PETO**
Falstaff!--Fast asleep behind the arras, and
snorting like a horse.
**PRINCE HENRY**
Hark, how hard he fetches breath. Search his pockets.
*He searcheth his pockets, and findeth certain papers*
What hast thou found?
**PETO**
Nothing but papers, my lord.
**PRINCE HENRY**
Let's see what they be: read them.
**PETO**
[Reads] Item, A capon,. . 2s. 2d.
Item, Sauce,. . . 4d.
Item, Sack, two gallons, 5s. 8d.
Item, Anchovies and sack after supper, 2s. 6d.
Item, Bread, ob.
**PRINCE HENRY**
O monstrous! but one half-penny-worth of bread to
this intolerable deal of sack! What there is else,
keep close; we'll read it at more advantage: there
let him sleep till day. I'll to the court in the
morning. We must all to the wars, and thy place
shall be honourable. I'll procure this fat rogue a

charge of foot; and I know his death will be a march of twelve-score. The money shall be paid back again with advantage. Be with me betimes in the morning; and so, good morrow, Peto.

*Exeunt*

**PETO**

Good morrow, good my lord.

## ACT III

**SCENE I. Bangor. The Archdeacon's house.**

*Enter HOTSPUR, WORCESTER, MORTIMER, and GLENDOWER*

**MORTIMER**

These promises are fair, the parties sure,
And our induction full of prosperous hope.

**HOTSPUR**

Lord Mortimer, and cousin Glendower,
Will you sit down?
And uncle Worcester: a plague upon it!
I have forgot the map.

**GLENDOWER**

No, here it is.
Sit, cousin Percy; sit, good cousin Hotspur,
For by that name as oft as Lancaster
Doth speak of you, his cheek looks pale and with
A rising sigh he wisheth you in heaven.

**HOTSPUR**

And you in hell, as oft as he hears Owen Glendower spoke of.

**GLENDOWER**

I cannot blame him: at my nativity
The front of heaven was full of fiery shapes,
Of burning cressets; and at my birth
The frame and huge foundation of the earth
Shaked like a coward.

**HOTSPUR**

Why, so it would have done at the same season, if
your mother's cat had but kittened, though yourself
had never been born.

**GLENDOWER**

I say the earth did shake when I was born.

**HOTSPUR**

And I say the earth was not of my mind,
If you suppose as fearing you it shook.

**GLENDOWER**

The heavens were all on fire, the earth did tremble.

**HOTSPUR**

O, then the earth shook to see the heavens on fire,
And not in fear of your nativity.
Diseased nature oftentimes breaks forth
In strange eruptions; oft the teeming earth
Is with a kind of colic pinch'd and vex'd
By the imprisoning of unruly wind
Within her womb; which, for enlargement striving,
Shakes the old beldam earth and topples down
Steeples and moss-grown towers. At your birth
Our grandam earth, having this distemperature,
In passion shook.

**GLENDOWER**

Cousin, of many men
I do not bear these crossings. Give me leave
To tell you once again that at my birth
The front of heaven was full of fiery shapes,
The goats ran from the mountains, and the herds
Were strangely clamorous to the frighted fields.
These signs have mark'd me extraordinary;
And all the courses of my life do show
I am not in the roll of common men.
Where is he living, clipp'd in with the sea
That chides the banks of England, Scotland, Wales,
Which calls me pupil, or hath read to me?
And bring him out that is but woman's son

Can trace me in the tedious ways of art
And hold me pace in deep experiments.

**HOTSPUR**

I think there's no man speaks better Welsh.
I'll to dinner.

**MORTIMER**

Peace, cousin Percy; you will make him mad.

**GLENDOWER**

I can call spirits from the vasty deep.

**HOTSPUR**

Why, so can I, or so can any man;
But will they come when you do call for them?

**GLENDOWER**

Why, I can teach you, cousin, to command
The devil.

**HOTSPUR**

And I can teach thee, coz, to shame the devil
By telling truth: tell truth and shame the devil.
If thou have power to raise him, bring him hither,
And I'll be sworn I have power to shame him hence.
O, while you live, tell truth and shame the devil!

**MORTIMER**

Come, come, no more of this unprofitable chat.

**GLENDOWER**

Three times hath Henry Bolingbroke made head
Against my power; thrice from the banks of Wye
And sandy-bottom'd Severn have I sent him
Bootless home and weather-beaten back.

**HOTSPUR**

Home without boots, and in foul weather too!
How 'scapes he agues, in the devil's name?

**GLENDOWER**

Come, here's the map: shall we divide our right
According to our threefold order ta'en?

**MORTIMER**

The archdeacon hath divided it
Into three limits very equally:
England, from Trent and Severn hitherto,
By south and east is to my part assign'd:
All westward, Wales beyond the Severn shore,
And all the fertile land within that bound,
To Owen Glendower: and, dear coz, to you
The remnant northward, lying off from Trent.
And our indentures tripartite are drawn;
Which being sealed interchangeably,
A business that this night may execute,
To-morrow, cousin Percy, you and I
And my good Lord of Worcester will set forth
To meet your father and the Scottish power,
As is appointed us, at Shrewsbury.
My father Glendower is not ready yet,
Not shall we need his help these fourteen days.
Within that space you may have drawn together
Your tenants, friends and neighbouring gentlemen.

**GLENDOWER**

A shorter time shall send me to you, lords:
And in my conduct shall your ladies come;
From whom you now must steal and take no leave,
For there will be a world of water shed
Upon the parting of your wives and you.

**HOTSPUR**

Methinks my moiety, north from Burton here,
In quantity equals not one of yours:

See how this river comes me cranking in,
And cuts me from the best of all my land
A huge half-moon, a monstrous cantle out.
I'll have the current in this place damm'd up;
And here the smug and silver Trent shall run
In a new channel, fair and evenly;
It shall not wind with such a deep indent,
To rob me of so rich a bottom here.
**GLENDOWER**
Not wind? it shall, it must; you see it doth.
**MORTIMER**
Yea, but
Mark how he bears his course, and runs me up
With like advantage on the other side;
Gelding the opposed continent as much
As on the other side it takes from you.
**EARL OF WORCESTER**
Yea, but a little charge will trench him here
And on this north side win this cape of land;
And then he runs straight and even.
**HOTSPUR**
I'll have it so: a little charge will do it.
**GLENDOWER**
I'll not have it alter'd.
**HOTSPUR**
Will not you?
**GLENDOWER**
No, nor you shall not.
**HOTSPUR**
Who shall say me nay?
**GLENDOWER**
Why, that will I.
**HOTSPUR**
Let me not understand you, then; speak it in Welsh.
**GLENDOWER**
I can speak English, lord, as well as you;
For I was train'd up in the English court;
Where, being but young, I framed to the harp
Many an English ditty lovely well
And gave the tongue a helpful ornament,
A virtue that was never seen in you.
**HOTSPUR**
Marry,
And I am glad of it with all my heart:
I had rather be a kitten and cry mew
Than one of these same metre ballad-mongers;
I had rather hear a brazen canstick turn'd,
Or a dry wheel grate on the axle-tree;
And that would set my teeth nothing on edge,
Nothing so much as mincing poetry:
'Tis like the forced gait of a shuffling nag.
**GLENDOWER**
Come, you shall have Trent turn'd.
**HOTSPUR**
I do not care: I'll give thrice so much land
To any well-deserving friend;
But in the way of bargain, mark ye me,
I'll cavil on the ninth part of a hair.
Are the indentures drawn? shall we be gone?
**GLENDOWER**
The moon shines fair; you may away by night:
I'll haste the writer and withal
Break with your wives of your departure hence:

I am afraid my daughter will run mad,
So much she doteth on her Mortimer.
*Exit GLENDOWER*
**MORTIMER**
Fie, cousin Percy! how you cross my father!
**HOTSPUR**
I cannot choose: sometime he angers me
With telling me of the mouldwarp and the ant,
Of the dreamer Merlin and his prophecies,
And of a dragon and a finless fish,
A clip-wing'd griffin and a moulten raven,
A couching lion and a ramping cat,
And such a deal of skimble-skamble stuff
As puts me from my faith. I tell you what;
He held me last night at least nine hours
In reckoning up the several devils' names
That were his lackeys: I cried 'hum,' and 'well, go to,'
But mark'd him not a word. O, he is as tedious
As a tired horse, a railing wife;
Worse than a smoky house: I had rather live
With cheese and garlic in a windmill, far,
Than feed on cates and have him talk to me
In any summer-house in Christendom.
**MORTIMER**
In faith, he is a worthy gentleman,
Exceedingly well read, and profited
In strange concealments, valiant as a lion
And as wondrous affable and as bountiful
As mines of India. Shall I tell you, cousin?
He holds your temper in a high respect
And curbs himself even of his natural scope
When you come 'cross his humour; faith, he does:
I warrant you, that man is not alive
Might so have tempted him as you have done,
Without the taste of danger and reproof:
But do not use it oft, let me entreat you.
**EARL OF WORCESTER**
In faith, my lord, you are too wilful-blame;
And since your coming hither have done enough
To put him quite beside his patience.
You must needs learn, lord, to amend this fault:
Though sometimes it show greatness, courage, blood,--
And that's the dearest grace it renders you,--
Yet oftentimes it doth present harsh rage,
Defect of manners, want of government,
Pride, haughtiness, opinion and disdain:
The least of which haunting a nobleman
Loseth men's hearts and leaves behind a stain
Upon the beauty of all parts besides,
Beguiling them of commendation.
**HOTSPUR**
Well, I am school'd: good manners be your speed!
Here come our wives, and let us take our leave.
*Re-enter GLENDOWER with the ladies*
**MORTIMER**
This is the deadly spite that angers me;
My wife can speak no English, I no Welsh.
**GLENDOWER**
My daughter weeps: she will not part with you;
She'll be a soldier too, she'll to the wars.
**MORTIMER**
Good father, tell her that she and my aunt Percy
Shall follow in your conduct speedily.

*Glendower speaks to her in Welsh, and she answers him in the same*
**GLENDOWER**
She is desperate here; a peevish self-wind harlotry,
one that no persuasion can do good upon.
*The lady speaks in Welsh*
**MORTIMER**
I understand thy looks: that pretty Welsh
Which thou pour'st down from these swelling heavens
I am too perfect in; and, but for shame,
In such a parley should I answer thee.
*The lady speaks again in Welsh*
I understand thy kisses and thou mine,
And that's a feeling disputation:
But I will never be a truant, love,
Till I have learned thy language; for thy tongue
Makes Welsh as sweet as ditties highly penn'd,
Sung by a fair queen in a summer's bower,
With ravishing division, to her lute.
**GLENDOWER**
Nay, if you melt, then will she run mad.
*The lady speaks again in Welsh*
**MORTIMER**
O, I am ignorance itself in this!
**GLENDOWER**
She bids you on the wanton rushes lay you down
And rest your gentle head upon her lap,
And she will sing the song that pleaseth you
And on your eyelids crown the god of sleep.
Charming your blood with pleasing heaviness,
Making such difference 'twixt wake and sleep
As is the difference betwixt day and night
The hour before the heavenly-harness'd team
Begins his golden progress in the east.
**MORTIMER**
With all my heart I'll sit and hear her sing:
By that time will our book, I think, be drawn
**GLENDOWER**
Do so;
And those musicians that shall play to you
Hang in the air a thousand leagues from hence,
And straight they shall be here: sit, and attend.
**HOTSPUR**
Come, Kate, thou art perfect in lying down: come,
quick, quick, that I may lay my head in thy lap.
**LADY PERCY**
Go, ye giddy goose.
*The music plays*
**HOTSPUR**
Now I perceive the devil understands Welsh;
And 'tis no marvel he is so humorous.
By'r lady, he is a good musician.
**LADY PERCY**
Then should you be nothing but musical for you are
altogether governed by humours. Lie still, ye thief,
and hear the lady sing in Welsh.
**HOTSPUR**
I had rather hear Lady, my brach, howl in Irish.
**LADY PERCY**
Wouldst thou have thy head broken?
**HOTSPUR**
No.
**LADY PERCY**
Then be still.

**HOTSPUR**
Neither;'tis a woman's fault.
**LADY PERCY**
Now God help thee!
**HOTSPUR**
To the Welsh lady's bed.
**LADY PERCY**
What's that?
**HOTSPUR**
Peace! she sings.
*Here the lady sings a Welsh song*
**HOTSPUR**
Come, Kate, I'll have your song too.
**LADY PERCY**
Not mine, in good sooth.
**HOTSPUR**
Not yours, in good sooth! Heart! you swear like a
comfit-maker's wife. 'Not you, in good sooth,' and
'as true as I live,' and 'as God shall mend me,' and
'as sure as day,'
And givest such sarcenet surety for thy oaths,
As if thou never walk'st further than Finsbury.
Swear me, Kate, like a lady as thou art,
A good mouth-filling oath, and leave 'in sooth,'
And such protest of pepper-gingerbread,
To velvet-guards and Sunday-citizens.
Come, sing.
**LADY PERCY**
I will not sing.
**HOTSPUR**
'Tis the next way to turn tailor, or be red-breast
teacher. An the indentures be drawn, I'll away
within these two hours; and so, come in when ye will.
*Exit*
**GLENDOWER**
Come, come, Lord Mortimer; you are as slow
As hot Lord Percy is on fire to go.
By this our book is drawn; we'll but seal,
And then to horse immediately.
**MORTIMER**
With all my heart.
*Exeunt*
**SCENE II. London. The palace.**
*Enter KING HENRY IV, PRINCE HENRY, and others*
**KING HENRY IV**
Lords, give us leave; the Prince of Wales and I
Must have some private conference; but be near at hand,
For we shall presently have need of you.
*Exeunt Lords*
I know not whether God will have it so,
For some displeasing service I have done,
That, in his secret doom, out of my blood
He'll breed revengement and a scourge for me;
But thou dost in thy passages of life
Make me believe that thou art only mark'd
For the hot vengeance and the rod of heaven
To punish my mistreadings. Tell me else,
Could such inordinate and low desires,
Such poor, such bare, such lewd, such mean attempts,
Such barren pleasures, rude society,
As thou art match'd withal and grafted to,
Accompany the greatness of thy blood
And hold their level with thy princely heart?

**PRINCE HENRY**
So please your majesty, I would I could
Quit all offences with as clear excuse
As well as I am doubtless I can purge
Myself of many I am charged withal:
Yet such extenuation let me beg,
As, in reproof of many tales devised,
which oft the ear of greatness needs must hear,
By smiling pick-thanks and base news-mongers,
I may, for some things true, wherein my youth
Hath faulty wander'd and irregular,
Find pardon on my true submission.
**KING HENRY IV**
God pardon thee! yet let me wonder, Harry,
At thy affections, which do hold a wing
Quite from the flight of all thy ancestors.
Thy place in council thou hast rudely lost.
Which by thy younger brother is supplied,
And art almost an alien to the hearts
Of all the court and princes of my blood:
The hope and expectation of thy time
Is ruin'd, and the soul of every man
Prophetically doth forethink thy fall.
Had I so lavish of my presence been,
So common-hackney'd in the eyes of men,
So stale and cheap to vulgar company,
Opinion, that did help me to the crown,
Had still kept loyal to possession
And left me in reputeless banishment,
A fellow of no mark nor likelihood.
By being seldom seen, I could not stir
But like a comet I was wonder'd at;
That men would tell their children 'This is he;'
Others would say 'Where, which is Bolingbroke?'
And then I stole all courtesy from heaven,
And dress'd myself in such humility
That I did pluck allegiance from men's hearts,
Loud shouts and salutations from their mouths,
Even in the presence of the crowned king.
Thus did I keep my person fresh and new;
My presence, like a robe pontifical,
Ne'er seen but wonder'd at: and so my state,
Seldom but sumptuous, showed like a feast
And won by rareness such solemnity.
The skipping king, he ambled up and down
With shallow jesters and rash bavin wits,
Soon kindled and soon burnt; carded his state,
Mingled his royalty with capering fools,
Had his great name profaned with their scorns
And gave his countenance, against his name,
To laugh at gibing boys and stand the push
Of every beardless vain comparative,
Grew a companion to the common streets,
Enfeoff'd himself to popularity;
That, being daily swallow'd by men's eyes,
They surfeited with honey and began
To loathe the taste of sweetness, whereof a little
More than a little is by much too much.
So when he had occasion to be seen,
He was but as the cuckoo is in June,
Heard, not regarded; seen, but with such eyes
As, sick and blunted with community,
Afford no extraordinary gaze,

Such as is bent on sun-like majesty
When it shines seldom in admiring eyes;
But rather drowzed and hung their eyelids down,
Slept in his face and render'd such aspect
As cloudy men use to their adversaries,
Being with his presence glutted, gorged and full.
And in that very line, Harry, standest thou;
For thou has lost thy princely privilege
With vile participation: not an eye
But is a-weary of thy common sight,
Save mine, which hath desired to see thee more;
Which now doth that I would not have it do,
Make blind itself with foolish tenderness.
**PRINCE HENRY**
I shall hereafter, my thrice gracious lord,
Be more myself.
**KING HENRY IV**
For all the world
As thou art to this hour was Richard then
When I from France set foot at Ravenspurgh,
And even as I was then is Percy now.
Now, by my sceptre and my soul to boot,
He hath more worthy interest to the state
Than thou the shadow of succession;
For of no right, nor colour like to right,
He doth fill fields with harness in the realm,
Turns head against the lion's armed jaws,
And, being no more in debt to years than thou,
Leads ancient lords and reverend bishops on
To bloody battles and to bruising arms.
What never-dying honour hath he got
Against renowned Douglas! whose high deeds,
Whose hot incursions and great name in arms
Holds from all soldiers chief majority
And military title capital
Through all the kingdoms that acknowledge Christ:
Thrice hath this Hotspur, Mars in swathling clothes,
This infant warrior, in his enterprises
Discomfited great Douglas, ta'en him once,
Enlarged him and made a friend of him,
To fill the mouth of deep defiance up
And shake the peace and safety of our throne.
And what say you to this? Percy, Northumberland,
The Archbishop's grace of York, Douglas, Mortimer,
Capitulate against us and are up.
But wherefore do I tell these news to thee?
Why, Harry, do I tell thee of my foes,
Which art my near'st and dearest enemy?
Thou that art like enough, through vassal fear,
Base inclination and the start of spleen
To fight against me under Percy's pay,
To dog his heels and curtsy at his frowns,
To show how much thou art degenerate.
**PRINCE HENRY**
Do not think so; you shall not find it so:
And God forgive them that so much have sway'd
Your majesty's good thoughts away from me!
I will redeem all this on Percy's head
And in the closing of some glorious day
Be bold to tell you that I am your son;
When I will wear a garment all of blood
And stain my favours in a bloody mask,
Which, wash'd away, shall scour my shame with it:

And that shall be the day, whene'er it lights,
That this same child of honour and renown,
This gallant Hotspur, this all-praised knight,
And your unthought-of Harry chance to meet.
For every honour sitting on his helm,
Would they were multitudes, and on my head
My shames redoubled! for the time will come,
That I shall make this northern youth exchange
His glorious deeds for my indignities.
Percy is but my factor, good my lord,
To engross up glorious deeds on my behalf;
And I will call him to so strict account,
That he shall render every glory up,
Yea, even the slightest worship of his time,
Or I will tear the reckoning from his heart.
This, in the name of God, I promise here:
The which if He be pleased I shall perform,
I do beseech your majesty may salve
The long-grown wounds of my intemperance:
If not, the end of life cancels all bands;
And I will die a hundred thousand deaths
Ere break the smallest parcel of this vow.

**KING HENRY IV**

A hundred thousand rebels die in this:
Thou shalt have charge and sovereign trust herein.
*Enter BLUNT*
How now, good Blunt? thy looks are full of speed.

**SIR WALTER BLUNT**

So hath the business that I come to speak of.
Lord Mortimer of Scotland hath sent word
That Douglas and the English rebels met
The eleventh of this month at Shrewsbury
A mighty and a fearful head they are,
If promises be kept on every hand,
As ever offer'd foul play in the state.

**KING HENRY IV**

The Earl of Westmoreland set forth to-day;
With him my son, Lord John of Lancaster;
For this advertisement is five days old:
On Wednesday next, Harry, you shall set forward;
On Thursday we ourselves will march: our meeting
Is Bridgenorth: and, Harry, you shall march
Through Gloucestershire; by which account,
Our business valued, some twelve days hence
Our general forces at Bridgenorth shall meet.
Our hands are full of business: let's away;
Advantage feeds him fat, while men delay.
*Exeunt*

**Scene III**

Eastcheap. The Boar's-Head Tavern.
*Enter FALSTAFF and BARDOLPH*

**FALSTAFF**

Bardolph, am I not fallen away vilely since this last
action? do I not bate? do I not dwindle? Why my
skin hangs about me like an like an old lady's loose
gown; I am withered like an old apple-john. Well,
I'll repent, and that suddenly, while I am in some
liking; I shall be out of heart shortly, and then I
shall have no strength to repent. An I have not
forgotten what the inside of a church is made of, I
am a peppercorn, a brewer's horse: the inside of a
church! Company, villanous company, hath been the
spoil of me.

**BARDOLPH**
Sir John, you are so fretful, you cannot live long.
**FALSTAFF**
Why, there is it: come sing me a bawdy song; make me merry. I was as virtuously given as a gentleman need to be; virtuous enough; swore little; diced not above seven times a week; went to a bawdy-house once in a quarter--of an hour; paid money that I borrowed, three of four times; lived well and in good compass: and now I live out of all order, out of all compass.
**BARDOLPH**
Why, you are so fat, Sir John, that you must needs be out of all compass, out of all reasonable compass, Sir John.
**FALSTAFF**
Do thou amend thy face, and I'll amend my life: thou art our admiral, thou bearest the lantern in the poop, but 'tis in the nose of thee; thou art the Knight of the Burning Lamp.
**BARDOLPH**
Why, Sir John, my face does you no harm.
**FALSTAFF**
No, I'll be sworn; I make as good use of it as many a man doth of a Death's-head or a memento mori: I never see thy face but I think upon hell-fire and Dives that lived in purple; for there he is in his robes, burning, burning. If thou wert any way given to virtue, I would swear by thy face; my oath should be 'By this fire, that's God's angel:' but thou art altogether given over; and wert indeed, but for the light in thy face, the son of utter darkness. When thou rannest up Gadshill in the night to catch my horse, if I did not think thou hadst been an ignis fatuus or a ball of wildfire, there's no purchase in money. O, thou art a perpetual triumph, an everlasting bonfire-light! Thou hast saved me a thousand marks in links and torches, walking with thee in the night betwixt tavern and tavern: but the sack that thou hast drunk me would have bought me lights as good cheap at the dearest chandler's in Europe. I have maintained that salamander of yours with fire any time this two and thirty years; God reward me for it!
**BARDOLPH**
'Sblood, I would my face were in your belly!
**FALSTAFF**
God-a-mercy! so should I be sure to be heart-burned.
*Enter Hostess*
How now, Dame Partlet the hen! have you inquired yet who picked my pocket?
**Hostess**
Why, Sir John, what do you think, Sir John? do you think I keep thieves in my house? I have searched, I have inquired, so has my husband, man by man, boy by boy, servant by servant: the tithe of a hair was never lost in my house before.
**FALSTAFF**
Ye lie, hostess: Bardolph was shaved and lost many a hair; and I'll be sworn my pocket was picked. Go to, you are a woman, go.
**Hostess**

Who, I? no; I defy thee: God's light, I was never
called so in mine own house before.

**FALSTAFF**

Go to, I know you well enough.

**Hostess**

No, Sir John; You do not know me, Sir John. I know
you, Sir John: you owe me money, Sir John; and now
you pick a quarrel to beguile me of it: I bought
you a dozen of shirts to your back.

**FALSTAFF**

Dowlas, filthy dowlas: I have given them away to
bakers' wives, and they have made bolters of them.

**Hostess**

Now, as I am a true woman, holland of eight
shillings an ell. You owe money here besides, Sir
John, for your diet and by-drinkings, and money lent
you, four and twenty pound.

**FALSTAFF**

He had his part of it; let him pay.

**Hostess**

He? alas, he is poor; he hath nothing.

**FALSTAFF**

How! poor? look upon his face; what call you rich?
let them coin his nose, let them coin his cheeks:
Ill not pay a denier. What, will you make a younker
of me? shall I not take mine ease in mine inn but I
shall have my pocket picked? I have lost a
seal-ring of my grandfather's worth forty mark.

**Hostess**

O Jesu, I have heard the prince tell him, I know not
how oft, that ring was copper!

**FALSTAFF**

How! the prince is a Jack, a sneak-cup: 'sblood, an
he were here, I would cudgel him like a dog, if he
would say so.

*Enter PRINCE HENRY and PETO, marching, and FALSTAFF meets them playing on his truncheon like a life*

How now, lad! is the wind in that door, i' faith?
must we all march?

**BARDOLPH**

Yea, two and two, Newgate fashion.

**Hostess**

My lord, I pray you, hear me.

**PRINCE HENRY**

What sayest thou, Mistress Quickly? How doth thy
husband? I love him well; he is an honest man.

**Hostess**

Good my lord, hear me.

**FALSTAFF**

Prithee, let her alone, and list to me.

**PRINCE HENRY**

What sayest thou, Jack?

**FALSTAFF**

The other night I fell asleep here behind the arras
and had my pocket picked: this house is turned
bawdy-house; they pick pockets.

**PRINCE HENRY**

What didst thou lose, Jack?

**FALSTAFF**

Wilt thou believe me, Hal? three or four bonds of
forty pound apiece, and a seal-ring of my
grandfather's.

**PRINCE HENRY**

A trifle, some eight-penny matter.

**Hostess**
So I told him, my lord; and I said I heard your grace say so: and, my lord, he speaks most vilely of you, like a foul-mouthed man as he is; and said he would cudgel you.
**PRINCE HENRY**
What! he did not?
**Hostess**
There's neither faith, truth, nor womanhood in me else.
**FALSTAFF**
There's no more faith in thee than in a stewed prune; nor no more truth in thee than in a drawn fox; and for womanhood, Maid Marian may be the deputy's wife of the ward to thee. Go, you thing, go
**Hostess**
Say, what thing? what thing?
**FALSTAFF**
What thing! why, a thing to thank God on.
**Hostess**
I am no thing to thank God on, I would thou shouldst know it; I am an honest man's wife: and, setting thy knighthood aside, thou art a knave to call me so.
**FALSTAFF**
Setting thy womanhood aside, thou art a beast to say otherwise.
**Hostess**
Say, what beast, thou knave, thou?
**FALSTAFF**
What beast! why, an otter.
**PRINCE HENRY**
An otter, Sir John! Why an otter?
**FALSTAFF**
Why, she's neither fish nor flesh; a man knows not where to have her.
**Hostess**
Thou art an unjust man in saying so: thou or any man knows where to have me, thou knave, thou!
**PRINCE HENRY**
Thou sayest true, hostess; and he slanders thee most grossly.
**Hostess**
So he doth you, my lord; and said this other day you ought him a thousand pound.
**PRINCE HENRY**
Sirrah, do I owe you a thousand pound?
**FALSTAFF**
A thousand pound, Ha! a million: thy love is worth a million: thou owest me thy love.
**Hostess**
Nay, my lord, he called you Jack, and said he would cudgel you.
**FALSTAFF**
Did I, Bardolph?
**BARDOLPH**
Indeed, Sir John, you said so.
**FALSTAFF**
Yea, if he said my ring was copper.
**PRINCE HENRY**
I say 'tis copper: darest thou be as good as thy word now?
**FALSTAFF**

Why, Hal, thou knowest, as thou art but man, I dare: but as thou art prince, I fear thee as I fear the roaring of a lion's whelp.
**PRINCE HENRY**
And why not as the lion?
**FALSTAFF**
The king is to be feared as the lion: dost thou think I'll fear thee as I fear thy father? nay, an I do, I pray God my girdle break.
**PRINCE HENRY**
O, if it should, how would thy guts fall about thy knees! But, sirrah, there's no room for faith, truth, nor honesty in this bosom of thine; it is all filled up with guts and midriff. Charge an honest woman with picking thy pocket! why, thou whoreson, impudent, embossed rascal, if there were anything in thy pocket but tavern-reckonings, memorandums of bawdy-houses, and one poor penny-worth of sugar-candy to make thee long-winded, if thy pocket were enriched with any other injuries but these, I am a villain: and yet you will stand to if; you will not pocket up wrong: art thou not ashamed?
**FALSTAFF**
Dost thou hear, Hal? thou knowest in the state of innocency Adam fell; and what should poor Jack Falstaff do in the days of villany? Thou seest I have more flesh than another man, and therefore more frailty. You confess then, you picked my pocket?
**PRINCE HENRY**
It appears so by the story.
**FALSTAFF**
Hostess, I forgive thee: go, make ready breakfast; love thy husband, look to thy servants, cherish thy guests: thou shalt find me tractable to any honest reason: thou seest I am pacified still. Nay, prithee, be gone.
*Exit Hostess*
Now Hal, to the news at court: for the robbery, lad, how is that answered?
**PRINCE HENRY**
O, my sweet beef, I must still be good angel to thee: the money is paid back again.
**FALSTAFF**
O, I do not like that paying back; 'tis a double labour.
**PRINCE HENRY**
I am good friends with my father and may do any thing.
**FALSTAFF**
Rob me the exchequer the first thing thou doest, and do it with unwashed hands too.
**BARDOLPH**
Do, my lord.
**PRINCE HENRY**
I have procured thee, Jack, a charge of foot.
**FALSTAFF**
I would it had been of horse. Where shall I find one that can steal well? O for a fine thief, of the age of two and twenty or thereabouts! I am heinously unprovided. Well, God be thanked for these rebels, they offend none but the virtuous: I laud them, I praise them.
**PRINCE HENRY**
Bardolph!
**BARDOLPH**

My lord?

**PRINCE HENRY**

Go bear this letter to Lord John of Lancaster, to my brother John; this to my Lord of Westmoreland.

*Exit Bardolph*

Go, Peto, to horse, to horse; for thou and I have thirty miles to ride yet ere dinner time.

*Exit Peto*

Jack, meet me to-morrow in the temple hall at two o'clock in the afternoon.

There shalt thou know thy charge; and there receive
Money and order for their furniture.
The land is burning; Percy stands on high;
And either we or they must lower lie.

*Exit PRINCE HENRY*

**FALSTAFF**

Rare words! brave world! Hostess, my breakfast, come!
O, I could wish this tavern were my drum!

*Exit*

## ACT IV

**SCENE I. The rebel camp near Shrewsbury.**

*Enter HOTSPUR, WORCESTER, and DOUGLAS*

**HOTSPUR**

Well said, my noble Scot: if speaking truth
In this fine age were not thought flattery,
Such attribution should the Douglas have,
As not a soldier of this season's stamp
Should go so general current through the world.
By God, I cannot flatter; I do defy
The tongues of soothers; but a braver place
In my heart's love hath no man than yourself:
Nay, task me to my word; approve me, lord.

**EARL OF DOUGLAS**

Thou art the king of honour:
No man so potent breathes upon the ground
But I will beard him.

**HOTSPUR**

Do so, and 'tis well.

*Enter a Messenger with letters*

What letters hast thou there?--I can but thank you.

**Messenger**

These letters come from your father.

**HOTSPUR**

Letters from him! why comes he not himself?

**Messenger**

He cannot come, my lord; he is grievous sick.

**HOTSPUR**

'Zounds! how has he the leisure to be sick
In such a rustling time? Who leads his power?
Under whose government come they along?

**Messenger**

His letters bear his mind, not I, my lord.

**EARL OF WORCESTER**

I prithee, tell me, doth he keep his bed?

**Messenger**

He did, my lord, four days ere I set forth;
And at the time of my departure thence
He was much fear'd by his physicians.

**EARL OF WORCESTER**

I would the state of time had first been whole
Ere he by sickness had been visited:
His health was never better worth than now.

**HOTSPUR**

Sick now! droop now! this sickness doth infect
The very life-blood of our enterprise;
'Tis catching hither, even to our camp.
He writes me here, that inward sickness--
And that his friends by deputation could not
So soon be drawn, nor did he think it meet
To lay so dangerous and dear a trust
On any soul removed but on his own.
Yet doth he give us bold advertisement,
That with our small conjunction we should on,
To see how fortune is disposed to us;
For, as he writes, there is no quailing now.
Because the king is certainly possess'd
Of all our purposes. What say you to it?

**EARL OF WORCESTER**

Your father's sickness is a maim to us.

**HOTSPUR**

A perilous gash, a very limb lopp'd off:
And yet, in faith, it is not; his present want

Seems more than we shall find it: were it good
To set the exact wealth of all our states
All at one cast? to set so rich a main
On the nice hazard of one doubtful hour?
It were not good; for therein should we read
The very bottom and the soul of hope,
The very list, the very utmost bound
Of all our fortunes.

**EARL OF DOUGLAS**

'Faith, and so we should;
Where now remains a sweet reversion:
We may boldly spend upon the hope of what
Is to come in:
A comfort of retirement lives in this.

**HOTSPUR**

A rendezvous, a home to fly unto.
If that the devil and mischance look big
Upon the maidenhead of our affairs.

**EARL OF WORCESTER**

But yet I would your father had been here.
The quality and hair of our attempt
Brooks no division: it will be thought
By some, that know not why he is away,
That wisdom, loyalty and mere dislike
Of our proceedings kept the earl from hence:
And think how such an apprehension
May turn the tide of fearful faction
And breed a kind of question in our cause;
For well you know we of the offering side
Must keep aloof from strict arbitrement,
And stop all sight-holes, every loop from whence
The eye of reason may pry in upon us:
This absence of your father's draws a curtain,
That shows the ignorant a kind of fear
Before not dreamt of.

**HOTSPUR**

You strain too far.
I rather of his absence make this use:
It lends a lustre and more great opinion,
A larger dare to our great enterprise,
Than if the earl were here; for men must think,
If we without his help can make a head
To push against a kingdom, with his help
We shall o'erturn it topsy-turvy down.
Yet all goes well, yet all our joints are whole.

**EARL OF DOUGLAS**

As heart can think: there is not such a word
Spoke of in Scotland as this term of fear.

*Enter SIR RICHARD VERNON*

**HOTSPUR**

My cousin Vernon, welcome, by my soul.

**VERNON**

Pray God my news be worth a welcome, lord.
The Earl of Westmoreland, seven thousand strong,
Is marching hitherwards; with him Prince John.

**HOTSPUR**

No harm: what more?

**VERNON**

And further, I have learn'd,
The king himself in person is set forth,
Or hitherwards intended speedily,
With strong and mighty preparation.

**HOTSPUR**

He shall be welcome too. Where is his son,
The nimble-footed madcap Prince of Wales,
And his comrades, that daff'd the world aside,
And bid it pass?

**VERNON**

All furnish'd, all in arms;
All plumed like estridges that with the wind
Baited like eagles having lately bathed;
Glittering in golden coats, like images;
As full of spirit as the month of May,
And gorgeous as the sun at midsummer;
Wanton as youthful goats, wild as young bulls.
I saw young Harry, with his beaver on,
His cuisses on his thighs, gallantly arm'd
Rise from the ground like feather'd Mercury,
And vaulted with such ease into his seat,
As if an angel dropp'd down from the clouds,
To turn and wind a fiery Pegasus
And witch the world with noble horsemanship.

**HOTSPUR**

No more, no more: worse than the sun in March,
This praise doth nourish agues. Let them come:
They come like sacrifices in their trim,
And to the fire-eyed maid of smoky war
All hot and bleeding will we offer them:
The mailed Mars shall on his altar sit
Up to the ears in blood. I am on fire
To hear this rich reprisal is so nigh
And yet not ours. Come, let me taste my horse,
Who is to bear me like a thunderbolt
Against the bosom of the Prince of Wales:
Harry to Harry shall, hot horse to horse,
Meet and ne'er part till one drop down a corse.
O that Glendower were come!

**VERNON**

There is more news:
I learn'd in Worcester, as I rode along,
He cannot draw his power this fourteen days.

**EARL OF DOUGLAS**

That's the worst tidings that I hear of yet.

**WORCESTER**

Ay, by my faith, that bears a frosty sound.

**HOTSPUR**

What may the king's whole battle reach unto?

**VERNON**

To thirty thousand.

**HOTSPUR**

Forty let it be:
My father and Glendower being both away,
The powers of us may serve so great a day
Come, let us take a muster speedily:
Doomsday is near; die all, die merrily.

**EARL OF DOUGLAS**

Talk not of dying: I am out of fear
Of death or death's hand for this one-half year.

*Exeunt*

**SCENE II. A public road near Coventry.**

*Enter FALSTAFF and BARDOLPH*

**FALSTAFF**

Bardolph, get thee before to Coventry; fill me a
bottle of sack: our soldiers shall march through;
we'll to Sutton Co'fil' tonight.

**BARDOLPH**

Will you give me money, captain?

**FALSTAFF**

Lay out, lay out.

**BARDOLPH**

This bottle makes an angel.

**FALSTAFF**

An if it do, take it for thy labour; and if it make
twenty, take them all; I'll answer the coinage. Bid
my lieutenant Peto meet me at town's end.

**BARDOLPH**

I will, captain: farewell.

*Exit*

**FALSTAFF**

If I be not ashamed of my soldiers, I am a soused
gurnet. I have misused the king's press damnably.
I have got, in exchange of a hundred and fifty
soldiers, three hundred and odd pounds. I press me
none but good house-holders, yeoman's sons; inquire
me out contracted bachelors, such as had been asked
twice on the banns; such a commodity of warm slaves,
as had as lieve hear the devil as a drum; such as
fear the report of a caliver worse than a struck
fowl or a hurt wild-duck. I pressed me none but such
toasts-and-butter, with hearts in their bellies no
bigger than pins' heads, and they have bought out
their services; and now my whole charge consists of
ancients, corporals, lieutenants, gentlemen of
companies, slaves as ragged as Lazarus in the
painted cloth, where the glutton's dogs licked his
sores; and such as indeed were never soldiers, but
discarded unjust serving-men, younger sons to
younger brothers, revolted tapsters and ostlers
trade-fallen, the cankers of a calm world and a
long peace, ten times more dishonourable ragged than
an old faced ancient: and such have I, to fill up
the rooms of them that have bought out their
services, that you would think that I had a hundred
and fifty tattered prodigals lately come from
swine-keeping, from eating draff and husks. A mad
fellow met me on the way and told me I had unloaded
all the gibbets and pressed the dead bodies. No eye
hath seen such scarecrows. I'll not march through
Coventry with them, that's flat: nay, and the
villains march wide betwixt the legs, as if they had
gyves on; for indeed I had the most of them out of
prison. There's but a shirt and a half in all my
company; and the half shirt is two napkins tacked
together and thrown over the shoulders like an
herald's coat without sleeves; and the shirt, to say
the truth, stolen from my host at Saint Alban's, or
the red-nose innkeeper of Daventry. But that's all
one; they'll find linen enough on every hedge.

*Enter the PRINCE and WESTMORELAND*

**PRINCE HENRY**

How now, blown Jack! how now, quilt!

**FALSTAFF**

What, Hal! how now, mad wag! what a devil dost thou
in Warwickshire? My good Lord of Westmoreland, I
cry you mercy: I thought your honour had already been
at Shrewsbury.

**WESTMORELAND**

Faith, Sir John,'tis more than time that I were
there, and you too; but my powers are there already.

The king, I can tell you, looks for us all: we must away all night.
**FALSTAFF**
Tut, never fear me: I am as vigilant as a cat to steal cream.
**PRINCE HENRY**
I think, to steal cream indeed, for thy theft hath already made thee butter. But tell me, Jack, whose fellows are these that come after?
**FALSTAFF**
Mine, Hal, mine.
**PRINCE HENRY**
I did never see such pitiful rascals.
**FALSTAFF**
Tut, tut; good enough to toss; food for powder, food for powder; they'll fill a pit as well as better: tush, man, mortal men, mortal men.
**WESTMORELAND**
Ay, but, Sir John, methinks they are exceeding poor and bare, too beggarly.
**FALSTAFF**
'Faith, for their poverty, I know not where they had that; and for their bareness, I am sure they never learned that of me.
**PRINCE HENRY**
No I'll be sworn; unless you call three fingers on the ribs bare. But, sirrah, make haste: Percy is already in the field.
**FALSTAFF**
What, is the king encamped?
**WESTMORELAND**
He is, Sir John: I fear we shall stay too long.
**FALSTAFF**
Well,
To the latter end of a fray and the beginning of a feast
Fits a dull fighter and a keen guest.
*Exeunt*
**SCENE III. The rebel camp near Shrewsbury.**
*Enter HOTSPUR, WORCESTER, DOUGLAS, and VERNON*
**HOTSPUR**
We'll fight with him to-night.
**EARL OF WORCESTER**
It may not be.
**EARL OF DOUGLAS**
You give him then the advantage.
**VERNON**
Not a whit.
**HOTSPUR**
Why say you so? looks he not for supply?
**VERNON**
So do we.
**HOTSPUR**
His is certain, ours is doubtful.
**EARL OF WORCESTER**
Good cousin, be advised; stir not tonight.
**VERNON**
Do not, my lord.
**EARL OF DOUGLAS**
You do not counsel well:
You speak it out of fear and cold heart.
**VERNON**
Do me no slander, Douglas: by my life,
And I dare well maintain it with my life,

If well-respected honour bid me on,
I hold as little counsel with weak fear
As you, my lord, or any Scot that this day lives:
Let it be seen to-morrow in the battle
Which of us fears.

**EARL OF DOUGLAS**

Yea, or to-night.

**VERNON**

Content.

**HOTSPUR**

To-night, say I.

**VERNON**

Come, come it nay not be. I wonder much,
Being men of such great leading as you are,
That you foresee not what impediments
Drag back our expedition: certain horse
Of my cousin Vernon's are not yet come up:
Your uncle Worcester's horse came but today;
And now their pride and mettle is asleep,
Their courage with hard labour tame and dull,
That not a horse is half the half of himself.

**HOTSPUR**

So are the horses of the enemy
In general, journey-bated and brought low:
The better part of ours are full of rest.

**EARL OF WORCESTER**

The number of the king exceedeth ours:
For God's sake. cousin, stay till all come in.

*The trumpet sounds a parley*

*Enter SIR WALTER BLUNT*

**SIR WALTER BLUNT**

I come with gracious offers from the king,
if you vouchsafe me hearing and respect.

**HOTSPUR**

Welcome, Sir Walter Blunt; and would to God
You were of our determination!
Some of us love you well; and even those some
Envy your great deservings and good name,
Because you are not of our quality,
But stand against us like an enemy.

**SIR WALTER BLUNT**

And God defend but still I should stand so,
So long as out of limit and true rule
You stand against anointed majesty.
But to my charge. The king hath sent to know
The nature of your griefs, and whereupon
You conjure from the breast of civil peace
Such bold hostility, teaching his duteous land
Audacious cruelty. If that the king
Have any way your good deserts forgot,
Which he confesseth to be manifold,
He bids you name your griefs; and with all speed
You shall have your desires with interest
And pardon absolute for yourself and these
Herein misled by your suggestion.

**HOTSPUR**

The king is kind; and well we know the king
Knows at what time to promise, when to pay.
My father and my uncle and myself
Did give him that same royalty he wears;
And when he was not six and twenty strong,
Sick in the world's regard, wretched and low,
A poor unminded outlaw sneaking home,

My father gave him welcome to the shore;
And when he heard him swear and vow to God
He came but to be Duke of Lancaster,
To sue his livery and beg his peace,
With tears of innocency and terms of zeal,
My father, in kind heart and pity moved,
Swore him assistance and perform'd it too.
Now when the lords and barons of the realm
Perceived Northumberland did lean to him,
The more and less came in with cap and knee;
Met him in boroughs, cities, villages,
Attended him on bridges, stood in lanes,
Laid gifts before him, proffer'd him their oaths,
Gave him their heirs, as pages follow'd him
Even at the heels in golden multitudes.
He presently, as greatness knows itself,
Steps me a little higher than his vow
Made to my father, while his blood was poor,
Upon the naked shore at Ravenspurgh;
And now, forsooth, takes on him to reform
Some certain edicts and some strait decrees
That lie too heavy on the commonwealth,
Cries out upon abuses, seems to weep
Over his country's wrongs; and by this face,
This seeming brow of justice, did he win
The hearts of all that he did angle for;
Proceeded further; cut me off the heads
Of all the favourites that the absent king
In deputation left behind him here,
When he was personal in the Irish war.
**SIR WALTER BLUNT**
Tut, I came not to hear this.
**HOTSPUR**
Then to the point.
In short time after, he deposed the king;
Soon after that, deprived him of his life;
And in the neck of that, task'd the whole state:
To make that worse, suffer'd his kinsman March,
Who is, if every owner were well placed,
Indeed his king, to be engaged in Wales,
There without ransom to lie forfeited;
Disgraced me in my happy victories,
Sought to entrap me by intelligence;
Rated mine uncle from the council-board;
In rage dismiss'd my father from the court;
Broke oath on oath, committed wrong on wrong,
And in conclusion drove us to seek out
This head of safety; and withal to pry
Into his title, the which we find
Too indirect for long continuance.
**SIR WALTER BLUNT**
Shall I return this answer to the king?
**HOTSPUR**
Not so, Sir Walter: we'll withdraw awhile.
Go to the king; and let there be impawn'd
Some surety for a safe return again,
And in the morning early shall my uncle
Bring him our purposes: and so farewell.
**SIR WALTER BLUNT**
I would you would accept of grace and love.
**HOTSPUR**
And may be so we shall.
**SIR WALTER BLUNT**

Pray God you do.
*Exeunt*
**SCENE IV. York. The ARCHBISHOP'S palace.**
*Enter the ARCHBISHOP OF YORK and SIR MICHAEL*
**ARCHBISHOP OF YORK**
Hie, good Sir Michael; bear this sealed brief
With winged haste to the lord marshal;
This to my cousin Scroop, and all the rest
To whom they are directed. If you knew
How much they do to import, you would make haste.
**SIR MICHAEL**
My good lord,
I guess their tenor.
**ARCHBISHOP OF YORK**
Like enough you do.
To-morrow, good Sir Michael, is a day
Wherein the fortune of ten thousand men
Must bide the touch; for, sir, at Shrewsbury,
As I am truly given to understand,
The king with mighty and quick-raised power
Meets with Lord Harry: and, I fear, Sir Michael,
What with the sickness of Northumberland,
Whose power was in the first proportion,
And what with Owen Glendower's absence thence,
Who with them was a rated sinew too
And comes not in, o'er-ruled by prophecies,
I fear the power of Percy is too weak
To wage an instant trial with the king.
**SIR MICHAEL**
Why, my good lord, you need not fear;
There is Douglas and Lord Mortimer.
**ARCHBISHOP OF YORK**
No, Mortimer is not there.
**SIR MICHAEL**
But there is Mordake, Vernon, Lord Harry Percy,
And there is my Lord of Worcester and a head
Of gallant warriors, noble gentlemen.
**ARCHBISHOP OF YORK**
And so there is: but yet the king hath drawn
The special head of all the land together:
The Prince of Wales, Lord John of Lancaster,
The noble Westmoreland and warlike Blunt;
And moe corrivals and dear men
Of estimation and command in arms.
**SIR MICHAEL**
Doubt not, my lord, they shall be well opposed.
**ARCHBISHOP OF YORK**
I hope no less, yet needful 'tis to fear;
And, to prevent the worst, Sir Michael, speed:
For if Lord Percy thrive not, ere the king
Dismiss his power, he means to visit us,
For he hath heard of our confederacy,
And 'tis but wisdom to make strong against him:
Therefore make haste. I must go write again
To other friends; and so farewell, Sir Michael.
*Exeunt*

## ACT V

**SCENE I. KING HENRY IV's camp near Shrewsbury.**

*Enter KING HENRY, PRINCE HENRY, Lord John of LANCASTER, EARL OF WESTMORELAND, SIR WALTER BLUNT, and FALSTAFF*

**KING HENRY IV**

How bloodily the sun begins to peer
Above yon busky hill! the day looks pale
At his distemperature.

**PRINCE HENRY**

The southern wind
Doth play the trumpet to his purposes,
And by his hollow whistling in the leaves
Foretells a tempest and a blustering day.

**KING HENRY IV**

Then with the losers let it sympathize,
For nothing can seem foul to those that win.
*The trumpet sounds*
*Enter WORCESTER and VERNON*
How now, my Lord of Worcester! 'tis not well
That you and I should meet upon such terms
As now we meet. You have deceived our trust,
And made us doff our easy robes of peace,
To crush our old limbs in ungentle steel:
This is not well, my lord, this is not well.
What say you to it? will you again unknit
This curlish knot of all-abhorred war?
And move in that obedient orb again
Where you did give a fair and natural light,
And be no more an exhaled meteor,
A prodigy of fear and a portent
Of broached mischief to the unborn times?

**EARL OF WORCESTER**

Hear me, my liege:
For mine own part, I could be well content
To entertain the lag-end of my life
With quiet hours; for I do protest,
I have not sought the day of this dislike.

**KING HENRY IV**

You have not sought it! how comes it, then?

**FALSTAFF**

Rebellion lay in his way, and he found it.

**PRINCE HENRY**

Peace, chewet, peace!

**EARL OF WORCESTER**

It pleased your majesty to turn your looks
Of favour from myself and all our house;
And yet I must remember you, my lord,
We were the first and dearest of your friends.
For you my staff of office did I break
In Richard's time; and posted day and night
to meet you on the way, and kiss your hand,
When yet you were in place and in account
Nothing so strong and fortunate as I.
It was myself, my brother and his son,
That brought you home and boldly did outdare
The dangers of the time. You swore to us,
And you did swear that oath at Doncaster,
That you did nothing purpose 'gainst the state;
Nor claim no further than your new-fall'n right,
The seat of Gaunt, dukedom of Lancaster:
To this we swore our aid. But in short space
It rain'd down fortune showering on your head;
And such a flood of greatness fell on you,

What with our help, what with the absent king,
What with the injuries of a wanton time,
The seeming sufferances that you had borne,
And the contrarious winds that held the king
So long in his unlucky Irish wars
That all in England did repute him dead:
And from this swarm of fair advantages
You took occasion to be quickly woo'd
To gripe the general sway into your hand;
Forget your oath to us at Doncaster;
And being fed by us you used us so
As that ungentle hull, the cuckoo's bird,
Useth the sparrow; did oppress our nest;
Grew by our feeding to so great a bulk
That even our love durst not come near your sight
For fear of swallowing; but with nimble wing
We were enforced, for safety sake, to fly
Out of sight and raise this present head;
Whereby we stand opposed by such means
As you yourself have forged against yourself
By unkind usage, dangerous countenance,
And violation of all faith and troth
Sworn to us in your younger enterprise.

**KING HENRY IV**

These things indeed you have articulate,
Proclaim'd at market-crosses, read in churches,
To face the garment of rebellion
With some fine colour that may please the eye
Of fickle changelings and poor discontents,
Which gape and rub the elbow at the news
Of hurlyburly innovation:
And never yet did insurrection want
Such water-colours to impaint his cause;
Nor moody beggars, starving for a time
Of pellmell havoc and confusion.

**PRINCE HENRY**

In both your armies there is many a soul
Shall pay full dearly for this encounter,
If once they join in trial. Tell your nephew,
The Prince of Wales doth join with all the world
In praise of Henry Percy: by my hopes,
This present enterprise set off his head,
I do not think a braver gentleman,
More active-valiant or more valiant-young,
More daring or more bold, is now alive
To grace this latter age with noble deeds.
For my part, I may speak it to my shame,
I have a truant been to chivalry;
And so I hear he doth account me too;
Yet this before my father's majesty--
I am content that he shall take the odds
Of his great name and estimation,
And will, to save the blood on either side,
Try fortune with him in a single fight.

**KING HENRY IV**

And, Prince of Wales, so dare we venture thee,
Albeit considerations infinite
Do make against it. No, good Worcester, no,
We love our people well; even those we love
That are misled upon your cousin's part;
And, will they take the offer of our grace,
Both he and they and you, every man
Shall be my friend again and I'll be his:

So tell your cousin, and bring me word
What he will do: but if he will not yield,
Rebuke and dread correction wait on us
And they shall do their office. So, be gone;
We will not now be troubled with reply:
We offer fair; take it advisedly.
*Exeunt WORCESTER and VERNON*
**PRINCE HENRY**
It will not be accepted, on my life:
The Douglas and the Hotspur both together
Are confident against the world in arms.
**KING HENRY IV**
Hence, therefore, every leader to his charge;
For, on their answer, will we set on them:
And God befriend us, as our cause is just!
*Exeunt all but PRINCE HENRY and FALSTAFF*
**FALSTAFF**
Hal, if thou see me down in the battle and bestride
me, so; 'tis a point of friendship.
**PRINCE HENRY**
Nothing but a colossus can do thee that friendship.
Say thy prayers, and farewell.
**FALSTAFF**
I would 'twere bed-time, Hal, and all well.
**PRINCE HENRY**
Why, thou owest God a death.
*Exit PRINCE HENRY*
**FALSTAFF**
'Tis not due yet; I would be loath to pay him before
his day. What need I be so forward with him that
calls not on me? Well, 'tis no matter; honour pricks
me on. Yea, but how if honour prick me off when I
come on? how then? Can honour set to a leg? no: or
an arm? no: or take away the grief of a wound? no.
Honour hath no skill in surgery, then? no. What is
honour? a word. What is in that word honour? what
is that honour? air. A trim reckoning! Who hath it?
he that died o' Wednesday. Doth he feel it? no.
Doth he hear it? no. 'Tis insensible, then. Yea,
to the dead. But will it not live with the living?
no. Why? detraction will not suffer it. Therefore
I'll none of it. Honour is a mere scutcheon: and so
ends my catechism.
*Exit*
**SCENE II. The rebel camp.**
*Enter WORCESTER and VERNON*
**EARL OF WORCESTER**
O, no, my nephew must not know, Sir Richard,
The liberal and kind offer of the king.
**VERNON**
'Twere best he did.
**EARL OF WORCESTER**
Then are we all undone.
It is not possible, it cannot be,
The king should keep his word in loving us;
He will suspect us still and find a time
To punish this offence in other faults:
Suspicion all our lives shall be stuck full of eyes;
For treason is but trusted like the fox,
Who, ne'er so tame, so cherish'd and lock'd up,
Will have a wild trick of his ancestors.
Look how we can, or sad or merrily,
Interpretation will misquote our looks,

And we shall feed like oxen at a stall,
The better cherish'd, still the nearer death.
My nephew's trespass may be well forgot;
it hath the excuse of youth and heat of blood,
And an adopted name of privilege,
A hair-brain'd Hotspur, govern'd by a spleen:
All his offences live upon my head
And on his father's; we did train him on,
And, his corruption being ta'en from us,
We, as the spring of all, shall pay for all.
Therefore, good cousin, let not Harry know,
In any case, the offer of the king.
**VERNON**
Deliver what you will; I'll say 'tis so.
Here comes your cousin.
*Enter HOTSPUR and DOUGLAS*
**HOTSPUR**
My uncle is return'd:
Deliver up my Lord of Westmoreland.
Uncle, what news?
**EARL OF WORCESTER**
The king will bid you battle presently.
**EARL OF DOUGLAS**
Defy him by the Lord of Westmoreland.
**HOTSPUR**
Lord Douglas, go you and tell him so.
**EARL OF DOUGLAS**
Marry, and shall, and very willingly.
*Exit*
**EARL OF WORCESTER**
There is no seeming mercy in the king.
**HOTSPUR**
Did you beg any? God forbid!
**EARL OF WORCESTER**
I told him gently of our grievances,
Of his oath-breaking; which he mended thus,
By now forswearing that he is forsworn:
He calls us rebels, traitors; and will scourge
With haughty arms this hateful name in us.
*Re-enter the EARL OF DOUGLAS*
**EARL OF DOUGLAS**
Arm, gentlemen; to arms! for I have thrown
A brave defiance in King Henry's teeth,
And Westmoreland, that was engaged, did bear it;
Which cannot choose but bring him quickly on.
**EARL OF WORCESTER**
The Prince of Wales stepp'd forth before the king,
And, nephew, challenged you to single fight.
**HOTSPUR**
O, would the quarrel lay upon our heads,
And that no man might draw short breath today
But I and Harry Monmouth! Tell me, tell me,
How show'd his tasking? seem'd it in contempt?
**VERNON**
No, by my soul; I never in my life
Did hear a challenge urged more modestly,
Unless a brother should a brother dare
To gentle exercise and proof of arms.
He gave you all the duties of a man;
Trimm'd up your praises with a princely tongue,
Spoke to your deservings like a chronicle,
Making you ever better than his praise
By still dispraising praise valued in you;

And, which became him like a prince indeed,
He made a blushing cital of himself;
And chid his truant youth with such a grace
As if he master'd there a double spirit.
Of teaching and of learning instantly.
There did he pause: but let me tell the world,
If he outlive the envy of this day,
England did never owe so sweet a hope,
So much misconstrued in his wantonness.
**HOTSPUR**
Cousin, I think thou art enamoured
On his follies: never did I hear
Of any prince so wild a libertine.
But be he as he will, yet once ere night
I will embrace him with a soldier's arm,
That he shall shrink under my courtesy.
Arm, arm with speed: and, fellows, soldiers, friends,
Better consider what you have to do
Than I, that have not well the gift of tongue,
Can lift your blood up with persuasion.
*Enter a Messenger*
**Messenger**
My lord, here are letters for you.
**HOTSPUR**
I cannot read them now.
O gentlemen, the time of life is short!
To spend that shortness basely were too long,
If life did ride upon a dial's point,
Still ending at the arrival of an hour.
An if we live, we live to tread on kings;
If die, brave death, when princes die with us!
Now, for our consciences, the arms are fair,
When the intent of bearing them is just.
*Enter another Messenger*
**Messenger**
My lord, prepare; the king comes on apace.
**HOTSPUR**
I thank him, that he cuts me from my tale,
For I profess not talking; only this--
Let each man do his best: and here draw I
A sword, whose temper I intend to stain
With the best blood that I can meet withal
In the adventure of this perilous day.
Now, Esperance! Percy! and set on.
Sound all the lofty instruments of war,
And by that music let us all embrace;
For, heaven to earth, some of us never shall
A second time do such a courtesy.
*The trumpets sound. They embrace, and exeunt*
**SCENE III. Plain between the camps.**
*KING HENRY enters with his power. Alarum to the battle. Then enter DOUGLAS and SIR WALTER BLUNT*
**SIR WALTER BLUNT**
What is thy name, that in the battle thus
Thou crossest me? what honour dost thou seek
Upon my head?
**EARL OF DOUGLAS**
Know then, my name is Douglas;
And I do haunt thee in the battle thus
Because some tell me that thou art a king.
**SIR WALTER BLUNT**
They tell thee true.
**EARL OF DOUGLAS**

The Lord of Stafford dear to-day hath bought
Thy likeness, for instead of thee, King Harry,
This sword hath ended him: so shall it thee,
Unless thou yield thee as my prisoner.
**SIR WALTER BLUNT**
I was not born a yielder, thou proud Scot;
And thou shalt find a king that will revenge
Lord Stafford's death.
*They fight. DOUGLAS kills SIR WALTER BLUNT. Enter HOTSPUR*
**HOTSPUR**
O Douglas, hadst thou fought at Holmedon thus,
never had triumph'd upon a Scot.
**EARL OF DOUGLAS**
All's done, all's won; here breathless lies the king.
**HOTSPUR**
Where?
**EARL OF DOUGLAS**
Here.
**HOTSPUR**
This, Douglas? no: I know this face full well:
A gallant knight he was, his name was Blunt;
Semblably furnish'd like the king himself.
**EARL OF DOUGLAS**
A fool go with thy soul, whither it goes!
A borrow'd title hast thou bought too dear:
Why didst thou tell me that thou wert a king?
**HOTSPUR**
The king hath many marching in his coats.
**EARL OF DOUGLAS**
Now, by my sword, I will kill all his coats;
I'll murder all his wardrobe, piece by piece,
Until I meet the king.
**HOTSPUR**
Up, and away!
Our soldiers stand full fairly for the day.
*Exeunt*
*Alarum. Enter FALSTAFF, solus*
**FALSTAFF**
Though I could 'scape shot-free at London, I fear
the shot here; here's no scoring but upon the pate.
Soft! who are you? Sir Walter Blunt: there's honour
for you! here's no vanity! I am as hot as moulten
lead, and as heavy too: God keep lead out of me! I
need no more weight than mine own bowels. I have
led my ragamuffins where they are peppered: there's
not three of my hundred and fifty left alive; and
they are for the town's end, to beg during life.
But who comes here?
*Enter PRINCE HENRY*
**PRINCE HENRY**
What, stand'st thou idle here? lend me thy sword:
Many a nobleman lies stark and stiff
Under the hoofs of vaunting enemies,
Whose deaths are yet unrevenged: I prithee,
lend me thy sword.
**FALSTAFF**
O Hal, I prithee, give me leave to breathe awhile.
Turk Gregory never did such deeds in arms as I have
done this day. I have paid Percy, I have made him sure.
**PRINCE HENRY**
He is, indeed; and living to kill thee. I prithee,
lend me thy sword.
**FALSTAFF**

Nay, before God, Hal, if Percy be alive, thou get'st
not my sword; but take my pistol, if thou wilt.

**PRINCE HENRY**

Give it to me: what, is it in the case?

**FALSTAFF**

Ay, Hal; 'tis hot, 'tis hot; there's that will sack a city.

*PRINCE HENRY draws it out, and finds it to be a bottle of sack*

**PRINCE HENRY**

What, is it a time to jest and dally now?

*He throws the bottle at him. Exit*

**FALSTAFF**

Well, if Percy be alive, I'll pierce him. If he do
come in my way, so: if he do not, if I come in his
willingly, let him make a carbonado of me. I like
not such grinning honour as Sir Walter hath: give me
life: which if I can save, so; if not, honour comes
unlooked for, and there's an end.

*Exit FALSTAFF*

**SCENE IV. Another part of the field.**

*Alarum. Excursions. Enter PRINCE HENRY, LORD JOHN OF LANCASTER, and EARL OF WESTMORELAND*

**KING HENRY IV**

I prithee,
Harry, withdraw thyself; thou bleed'st too much.
Lord John of Lancaster, go you with him.

**LANCASTER**

Not I, my lord, unless I did bleed too.

**PRINCE HENRY**

I beseech your majesty, make up,
Lest your retirement do amaze your friends.

**KING HENRY IV**

I will do so.
My Lord of Westmoreland, lead him to his tent.

**WESTMORELAND**

Come, my lord, I'll lead you to your tent.

**PRINCE HENRY**

Lead me, my lord? I do not need your help:
And God forbid a shallow scratch should drive
The Prince of Wales from such a field as this,
Where stain'd nobility lies trodden on,
and rebels' arms triumph in massacres!

**LANCASTER**

We breathe too long: come, cousin Westmoreland,
Our duty this way lies; for God's sake come.

*Exeunt LANCASTER and WESTMORELAND*

**PRINCE HENRY**

By God, thou hast deceived me, Lancaster;
I did not think thee lord of such a spirit:
Before, I loved thee as a brother, John;
But now, I do respect thee as my soul.

**KING HENRY IV**

I saw him hold Lord Percy at the point
With lustier maintenance than I did look for
Of such an ungrown warrior.

**PRINCE HENRY**

O, this boy
Lends mettle to us all!

*Exit*

*Enter DOUGLAS*

**EARL OF DOUGLAS**

Another king! they grow like Hydra's heads:
I am the Douglas, fatal to all those

That wear those colours on them: what art thou,
That counterfeit'st the person of a king?
**KING HENRY IV**
The king himself; who, Douglas, grieves at heart
So many of his shadows thou hast met
And not the very king. I have two boys
Seek Percy and thyself about the field:
But, seeing thou fall'st on me so luckily,
I will assay thee: so, defend thyself.
**EARL OF DOUGLAS**
I fear thou art another counterfeit;
And yet, in faith, thou bear'st thee like a king:
But mine I am sure thou art, whoe'er thou be,
And thus I win thee.
*They fight. KING HENRY being in danger, PRINCE HENRY enters*
**PRINCE HENRY**
Hold up thy head, vile Scot, or thou art like
Never to hold it up again! the spirits
Of valiant Shirley, Stafford, Blunt, are in my arms:
It is the Prince of Wales that threatens thee;
Who never promiseth but he means to pay.
*They fight: DOUGLAS flies*
Cheerly, my lord how fares your grace?
Sir Nicholas Gawsey hath for succor sent,
And so hath Clifton: I'll to Clifton straight.
**KING HENRY IV**
Stay, and breathe awhile:
Thou hast redeem'd thy lost opinion,
And show'd thou makest some tender of my life,
In this fair rescue thou hast brought to me.
**PRINCE HENRY**
O God! they did me too much injury
That ever said I hearken'd for your death.
If it were so, I might have let alone
The insulting hand of Douglas over you,
Which would have been as speedy in your end
As all the poisonous potions in the world
And saved the treacherous labour of your son.
**KING HENRY IV**
Make up to Clifton: I'll to Sir Nicholas Gawsey.
*Exit*
*Enter HOTSPUR*
**HOTSPUR**
If I mistake not, thou art Harry Monmouth.
**PRINCE HENRY**
Thou speak'st as if I would deny my name.
**HOTSPUR**
My name is Harry Percy.
**PRINCE HENRY**
Why, then I see
A very valiant rebel of the name.
I am the Prince of Wales; and think not, Percy,
To share with me in glory any more:
Two stars keep not their motion in one sphere;
Nor can one England brook a double reign,
Of Harry Percy and the Prince of Wales.
**HOTSPUR**
Nor shall it, Harry; for the hour is come
To end the one of us; and would to God
Thy name in arms were now as great as mine!
**PRINCE HENRY**

I'll make it greater ere I part from thee;
And all the budding honours on thy crest
I'll crop, to make a garland for my head.
**HOTSPUR**
I can no longer brook thy vanities.
*They fight*
*Enter FALSTAFF*
**FALSTAFF**
Well said, Hal! to it Hal! Nay, you shall find no
boy's play here, I can tell you.
*Re-enter DOUGLAS; he fights with FALSTAFF, who falls down as if he were dead, and exit DOUGLAS. HOTSPUR is wounded, and falls*
**HOTSPUR**
O, Harry, thou hast robb'd me of my youth!
I better brook the loss of brittle life
Than those proud titles thou hast won of me;
They wound my thoughts worse than sword my flesh:
But thought's the slave of life, and life time's fool;
And time, that takes survey of all the world,
Must have a stop. O, I could prophesy,
But that the earthy and cold hand of death
Lies on my tongue: no, Percy, thou art dust
And food for--
*Dies*
**PRINCE HENRY**
For worms, brave Percy: fare thee well, great heart!
Ill-weaved ambition, how much art thou shrunk!
When that this body did contain a spirit,
A kingdom for it was too small a bound;
But now two paces of the vilest earth
Is room enough: this earth that bears thee dead
Bears not alive so stout a gentleman.
If thou wert sensible of courtesy,
I should not make so dear a show of zeal:
But let my favours hide thy mangled face;
And, even in thy behalf, I'll thank myself
For doing these fair rites of tenderness.
Adieu, and take thy praise with thee to heaven!
Thy ignominy sleep with thee in the grave,
But not remember'd in thy epitaph!
*He spieth FALSTAFF on the ground*
What, old acquaintance! could not all this flesh
Keep in a little life? Poor Jack, farewell!
I could have better spared a better man:
O, I should have a heavy miss of thee,
If I were much in love with vanity!
Death hath not struck so fat a deer to-day,
Though many dearer, in this bloody fray.
Embowell'd will I see thee by and by:
Till then in blood by noble Percy lie.
*Exit PRINCE HENRY*
**FALSTAFF**
[Rising up] Embowelled! if thou embowel me to-day,
I'll give you leave to powder me and eat me too
to-morrow. 'Sblood,'twas time to counterfeit, or
that hot termagant Scot had paid me scot and lot too.
Counterfeit? I lie, I am no counterfeit: to die,
is to be a counterfeit; for he is but the
counterfeit of a man who hath not the life of a man:
but to counterfeit dying, when a man thereby
liveth, is to be no counterfeit, but the true and
perfect image of life indeed. The better part of
valour is discretion; in the which better part I

have saved my life.'Zounds, I am afraid of this
gunpowder Percy, though he be dead: how, if he
should counterfeit too and rise? by my faith, I am
afraid he would prove the better counterfeit.
Therefore I'll make him sure; yea, and I'll swear I
killed him. Why may not he rise as well as I?
Nothing confutes me but eyes, and nobody sees me.
Therefore, sirrah,
*Stabbing him*
with a new wound in your thigh, come you along with me.
*Takes up HOTSPUR on his back*
*Re-enter PRINCE HENRY and LORD JOHN OF LANCASTER*
**PRINCE HENRY**
Come, brother John; full bravely hast thou flesh'd
Thy maiden sword.
**LANCASTER**
But, soft! whom have we here?
Did you not tell me this fat man was dead?
**PRINCE HENRY**
I did; I saw him dead,
Breathless and bleeding on the ground. Art
thou alive?
Or is it fantasy that plays upon our eyesight?
I prithee, speak; we will not trust our eyes
Without our ears: thou art not what thou seem'st.
**FALSTAFF**
No, that's certain; I am not a double man: but if I
be not Jack Falstaff, then am I a Jack. There is Percy:
*Throwing the body down*
if your father will do me any honour, so; if not, let
him kill the next Percy himself. I look to be either
earl or duke, I can assure you.
**PRINCE HENRY**
Why, Percy I killed myself and saw thee dead.
**FALSTAFF**
Didst thou? Lord, Lord, how this world is given to
lying! I grant you I was down and out of breath;
and so was he: but we rose both at an instant and
fought a long hour by Shrewsbury clock. If I may be
believed, so; if not, let them that should reward
valour bear the sin upon their own heads. I'll take
it upon my death, I gave him this wound in the
thigh: if the man were alive and would deny it,
'zounds, I would make him eat a piece of my sword.
**LANCASTER**
This is the strangest tale that ever I heard.
**PRINCE HENRY**
This is the strangest fellow, brother John.
Come, bring your luggage nobly on your back:
For my part, if a lie may do thee grace,
I'll gild it with the happiest terms I have.
*A retreat is sounded*
The trumpet sounds retreat; the day is ours.
Come, brother, let us to the highest of the field,
To see what friends are living, who are dead.
*Exeunt PRINCE HENRY and LANCASTER*
**FALSTAFF**
I'll follow, as they say, for reward. He that
rewards me, God reward him! If I do grow great,
I'll grow less; for I'll purge, and leave sack, and
live cleanly as a nobleman should do.
*Exit*
**SCENE V. Another part of the field.**

*The trumpets sound. Enter KING HENRY IV, PRINCE HENRY, LORD JOHN LANCASTER, EARL OF WESTMORELAND, with WORCESTER and VERNON prisoners*

**KING HENRY IV**

Thus ever did rebellion find rebuke.
Ill-spirited Worcester! did not we send grace,
Pardon and terms of love to all of you?
And wouldst thou turn our offers contrary?
Misuse the tenor of thy kinsman's trust?
Three knights upon our party slain to-day,
A noble earl and many a creature else
Had been alive this hour,
If like a Christian thou hadst truly borne
Betwixt our armies true intelligence.

**EARL OF WORCESTER**

What I have done my safety urged me to;
And I embrace this fortune patiently,
Since not to be avoided it falls on me.

**KING HENRY IV**

Bear Worcester to the death and Vernon too:
Other offenders we will pause upon.
*Exeunt WORCESTER and VERNON, guarded*
How goes the field?

**PRINCE HENRY**

The noble Scot, Lord Douglas, when he saw
The fortune of the day quite turn'd from him,
The noble Percy slain, and all his men
Upon the foot of fear, fled with the rest;
And falling from a hill, he was so bruised
That the pursuers took him. At my tent
The Douglas is; and I beseech your grace
I may dispose of him.

**KING HENRY IV**

With all my heart.

**PRINCE HENRY**

Then, brother John of Lancaster, to you
This honourable bounty shall belong:
Go to the Douglas, and deliver him
Up to his pleasure, ransomless and free:
His valour shown upon our crests to-day
Hath taught us how to cherish such high deeds
Even in the bosom of our adversaries.

**LANCASTER**

I thank your grace for this high courtesy,
Which I shall give away immediately.

**KING HENRY IV**

Then this remains, that we divide our power.
You, son John, and my cousin Westmoreland
Towards York shall bend you with your dearest speed,
To meet Northumberland and the prelate Scroop,
Who, as we hear, are busily in arms:
Myself and you, son Harry, will towards Wales,
To fight with Glendower and the Earl of March.
Rebellion in this land shall lose his sway,
Meeting the cheque of such another day:
And since this business so fair is done,
Let us not leave till all our own be won.
*Exeunt*

**End Part 1**

## Dramatis Personae

Rumour, *the Presenter*
King Henry the Fourth
Henry, Prince of Wales, *afterwards King Henry V*
Thomas, Duke of Clarence, *son of Henry the Fourth*
Prince John of Lancaster, *son of Henry the Fourth*
Prince Humphrey of Gloucester, *son of Henry the Fourth*
Earl of Warwick
Earl of Westmoreland
Earl of Surrey
Gower
Harcourt
Blunt
Lord Chief-Justice of the King's Bench
A Servant of the Chief-Justice
Earl of Northumberland
Scroop, Archbishop of York
Lord Mowbray
Lord Hastings
Lord Bardolph
Sir John Colevile
Travers and Morton, *retainers of Northumberland*
Sir John Falstaff
His Page
Bardolph
Pistol
Poins
Peto
Shallow, Silence, *country justices*
Davy, *Servant to Shallow*
Mouldy, Shadow, Wart, Feeble, and Bullcalf, recruits
Fang and Snare, *sheriff's officers*
Lady Northumberland
Lady Percy
Mistress Quickly, *hostess of a tavern in Eastcheap*
Doll Tearsheet
Lords and Attendants; Porter, Drawers, Beadles, Grooms, etc.
A Dancer, *speaker of the epilogue*

**None**

*Warkworth. Before the castle*

*Enter RUMOUR, painted full of tongues*

**RUMOUR**

Open your ears; for which of you will stop
The vent of hearing when loud Rumour speaks?
I, from the orient to the drooping west,
Making the wind my post-horse, still unfold
The acts commenced on this ball of earth:
Upon my tongues continual slanders ride,
The which in every language I pronounce,
Stuffing the ears of men with false reports.
I speak of peace, while covert enmity
Under the smile of safety wounds the world:
And who but Rumour, who but only I,
Make fearful musters and prepared defence,
Whiles the big year, swoln with some other grief,
Is thought with child by the stern tyrant war,
And no such matter? Rumour is a pipe
Blown by surmises, jealousies, conjectures
And of so easy and so plain a stop
That the blunt monster with uncounted heads,
The still-discordant wavering multitude,
Can play upon it. But what need I thus
My well-known body to anatomize
Among my household? Why is Rumour here?
I run before King Harry's victory;
Who in a bloody field by Shrewsbury
Hath beaten down young Hotspur and his troops,
Quenching the flame of bold rebellion
Even with the rebel's blood. But what mean I
To speak so true at first? my office is
To noise abroad that Harry Monmouth fell
Under the wrath of noble Hotspur's sword,
And that the king before the Douglas' rage
Stoop'd his anointed head as low as death.
This have I rumour'd through the peasant towns
Between that royal field of Shrewsbury
And this worm-eaten hold of ragged stone,
Where Hotspur's father, old Northumberland,
Lies crafty-sick: the posts come tiring on,
And not a man of them brings other news
Than they have learn'd of me: from Rumour's tongues
They bring smooth comforts false, worse than
true wrongs.

*Exit*

**SCENE I. The same.**
*Enter LORD BARDOLPH*
**LORD BARDOLPH**
Who keeps the gate here, ho?
*The Porter opens the gate*
Where is the earl?
**Porter**
What shall I say you are?
**LORD BARDOLPH**
Tell thou the earl
That the Lord Bardolph doth attend him here.
**Porter**
His lordship is walk'd forth into the orchard;
Please it your honour, knock but at the gate,
And he himself wilt answer.
*Enter NORTHUMBERLAND*
**LORD BARDOLPH**
Here comes the earl.
*Exit Porter*
**NORTHUMBERLAND**
What news, Lord Bardolph? every minute now
Should be the father of some stratagem:
The times are wild: contention, like a horse
Full of high feeding, madly hath broke loose
And bears down all before him.
**LORD BARDOLPH**
Noble earl,
I bring you certain news from Shrewsbury.
**NORTHUMBERLAND**
Good, an God will!
**LORD BARDOLPH**
As good as heart can wish:
The king is almost wounded to the death;
And, in the fortune of my lord your son,
Prince Harry slain outright; and both the Blunts
Kill'd by the hand of Douglas; young Prince John
And Westmoreland and Stafford fled the field;
And Harry Monmouth's brawn, the hulk Sir John,
Is prisoner to your son: O, such a day,
So fought, so follow'd and so fairly won,
Came not till now to dignify the times,
Since Caesar's fortunes!
**NORTHUMBERLAND**
How is this derived?
Saw you the field? came you from Shrewsbury?
**LORD BARDOLPH**
I spake with one, my lord, that came from thence,
A gentleman well bred and of good name,
That freely render'd me these news for true.
**NORTHUMBERLAND**
Here comes my servant Travers, whom I sent
On Tuesday last to listen after news.
*Enter TRAVERS*
**LORD BARDOLPH**
My lord, I over-rode him on the way;
And he is furnish'd with no certainties
More than he haply may retail from me.
**NORTHUMBERLAND**
Now, Travers, what good tidings comes with you?
**TRAVERS**
My lord, Sir John Umfrevile turn'd me back
With joyful tidings; and, being better horsed,

Out-rode me. After him came spurring hard
A gentleman, almost forspent with speed,
That stopp'd by me to breathe his bloodied horse.
He ask'd the way to Chester; and of him
I did demand what news from Shrewsbury:
He told me that rebellion had bad luck
And that young Harry Percy's spur was cold.
With that, he gave his able horse the head,
And bending forward struck his armed heels
Against the panting sides of his poor jade
Up to the rowel-head, and starting so
He seem'd in running to devour the way,
Staying no longer question.
**NORTHUMBERLAND**
Ha! Again:
Said he young Harry Percy's spur was cold?
Of Hotspur Coldspur? that rebellion
Had met ill luck?
**LORD BARDOLPH**
My lord, I'll tell you what;
If my young lord your son have not the day,
Upon mine honour, for a silken point
I'll give my barony: never talk of it.
**NORTHUMBERLAND**
Why should that gentleman that rode by Travers
Give then such instances of loss?
**LORD BARDOLPH**
Who, he?
He was some hilding fellow that had stolen
The horse he rode on, and, upon my life,
Spoke at a venture. Look, here comes more news.
*Enter MORTON*
**NORTHUMBERLAND**
Yea, this man's brow, like to a title-leaf,
Foretells the nature of a tragic volume:
So looks the strand whereon the imperious flood
Hath left a witness'd usurpation.
Say, Morton, didst thou come from Shrewsbury?
**MORTON**
I ran from Shrewsbury, my noble lord;
Where hateful death put on his ugliest mask
To fright our party.
**NORTHUMBERLAND**
How doth my son and brother?
Thou tremblest; and the whiteness in thy cheek
Is apter than thy tongue to tell thy errand.
Even such a man, so faint, so spiritless,
So dull, so dead in look, so woe-begone,
Drew Priam's curtain in the dead of night,
And would have told him half his Troy was burnt;
But Priam found the fire ere he his tongue,
And I my Percy's death ere thou report'st it.
This thou wouldst say, 'Your son did thus and thus;
Your brother thus: so fought the noble Douglas:'
Stopping my greedy ear with their bold deeds:
But in the end, to stop my ear indeed,
Thou hast a sigh to blow away this praise,
Ending with 'Brother, son, and all are dead.'
**MORTON**
Douglas is living, and your brother, yet;
But, for my lord your son--
**NORTHUMBERLAND**

Why, he is dead.
See what a ready tongue suspicion hath!
He that but fears the thing he would not know
Hath by instinct knowledge from others' eyes
That what he fear'd is chanced. Yet speak, Morton;
Tell thou an earl his divination lies,
And I will take it as a sweet disgrace
And make thee rich for doing me such wrong.
**MORTON**
You are too great to be by me gainsaid:
Your spirit is too true, your fears too certain.
**NORTHUMBERLAND**
Yet, for all this, say not that Percy's dead.
I see a strange confession in thine eye:
Thou shakest thy head and hold'st it fear or sin
To speak a truth. If he be slain, say so;
The tongue offends not that reports his death:
And he doth sin that doth belie the dead,
Not he which says the dead is not alive.
Yet the first bringer of unwelcome news
Hath but a losing office, and his tongue
Sounds ever after as a sullen bell,
Remember'd tolling a departing friend.
**LORD BARDOLPH**
I cannot think, my lord, your son is dead.
**MORTON**
I am sorry I should force you to believe
That which I would to God I had not seen;
But these mine eyes saw him in bloody state,
Rendering faint quittance, wearied and out-breathed,
To Harry Monmouth; whose swift wrath beat down
The never-daunted Percy to the earth,
From whence with life he never more sprung up.
In few, his death, whose spirit lent a fire
Even to the dullest peasant in his camp,
Being bruited once, took fire and heat away
From the best temper'd courage in his troops;
For from his metal was his party steel'd;
Which once in him abated, all the rest
Turn'd on themselves, like dull and heavy lead:
And as the thing that's heavy in itself,
Upon enforcement flies with greatest speed,
So did our men, heavy in Hotspur's loss,
Lend to this weight such lightness with their fear
That arrows fled not swifter toward their aim
Than did our soldiers, aiming at their safety,
Fly from the field. Then was the noble Worcester
Too soon ta'en prisoner; and that furious Scot,
The bloody Douglas, whose well-labouring sword
Had three times slain the appearance of the king,
'Gan vail his stomach and did grace the shame
Of those that turn'd their backs, and in his flight,
Stumbling in fear, was took. The sum of all
Is that the king hath won, and hath sent out
A speedy power to encounter you, my lord,
Under the conduct of young Lancaster
And Westmoreland. This is the news at full.
**NORTHUMBERLAND**
For this I shall have time enough to mourn.
In poison there is physic; and these news,
Having been well, that would have made me sick,
Being sick, have in some measure made me well:
And as the wretch, whose fever-weaken'd joints,

Like strengthless hinges, buckle under life,
Impatient of his fit, breaks like a fire
Out of his keeper's arms, even so my limbs,
Weaken'd with grief, being now enraged with grief,
Are thrice themselves. Hence, therefore, thou nice crutch!
A scaly gauntlet now with joints of steel
Must glove this hand: and hence, thou sickly quoif!
Thou art a guard too wanton for the head
Which princes, flesh'd with conquest, aim to hit.
Now bind my brows with iron; and approach
The ragged'st hour that time and spite dare bring
To frown upon the enraged Northumberland!
Let heaven kiss earth! now let not Nature's hand
Keep the wild flood confined! let order die!
And let this world no longer be a stage
To feed contention in a lingering act;
But let one spirit of the first-born Cain
Reign in all bosoms, that, each heart being set
On bloody courses, the rude scene may end,
And darkness be the burier of the dead!
**TRAVERS**
This strained passion doth you wrong, my lord.
**LORD BARDOLPH**
Sweet earl, divorce not wisdom from your honour.
**MORTON**
The lives of all your loving complices
Lean on your health; the which, if you give o'er
To stormy passion, must perforce decay.
You cast the event of war, my noble lord,
And summ'd the account of chance, before you said
'Let us make head.' It was your presurmise,
That, in the dole of blows, your son might drop:
You knew he walk'd o'er perils, on an edge,
More likely to fall in than to get o'er;
You were advised his flesh was capable
Of wounds and scars and that his forward spirit
Would lift him where most trade of danger ranged:
Yet did you say 'Go forth;' and none of this,
Though strongly apprehended, could restrain
The stiff-borne action: what hath then befallen,
Or what hath this bold enterprise brought forth,
More than that being which was like to be?
**LORD BARDOLPH**
We all that are engaged to this loss
Knew that we ventured on such dangerous seas
That if we wrought our life 'twas ten to one;
And yet we ventured, for the gain proposed
Choked the respect of likely peril fear'd;
And since we are o'erset, venture again.
Come, we will all put forth, body and goods.
**MORTON**
'Tis more than time: and, my most noble lord,
I hear for certain, and do speak the truth,
The gentle Archbishop of York is up
With well-appointed powers: he is a man
Who with a double surety binds his followers.
My lord your son had only but the corpse,
But shadows and the shows of men, to fight;
For that same word, rebellion, did divide
The action of their bodies from their souls;
And they did fight with queasiness, constrain'd,
As men drink potions, that their weapons only
Seem'd on our side; but, for their spirits and souls,

This word, rebellion, it had froze them up,
As fish are in a pond. But now the bishop
Turns insurrection to religion:
Supposed sincere and holy in his thoughts,
He's followed both with body and with mind;
And doth enlarge his rising with the blood
Of fair King Richard, scraped from Pomfret stones;
Derives from heaven his quarrel and his cause;
Tells them he doth bestride a bleeding land,
Gasping for life under great Bolingbroke;
And more and less do flock to follow him.

**NORTHUMBERLAND**

I knew of this before; but, to speak truth,
This present grief had wiped it from my mind.
Go in with me; and counsel every man
The aptest way for safety and revenge:
Get posts and letters, and make friends with speed:
Never so few, and never yet more need.

*Exeunt*

**SCENE II. London. A street.**

*Enter FALSTAFF, with his Page bearing his sword and buckler*

**FALSTAFF**

Sirrah, you giant, what says the doctor to my water?

**Page**

He said, sir, the water itself was a good healthy
water; but, for the party that owed it, he might
have more diseases than he knew for.

**FALSTAFF**

Men of all sorts take a pride to gird at me: the
brain of this foolish-compounded clay, man, is not
able to invent anything that tends to laughter, more
than I invent or is invented on me: I am not only
witty in myself, but the cause that wit is in other
men. I do here walk before thee like a sow that
hath overwhelmed all her litter but one. If the
prince put thee into my service for any other reason
than to set me off, why then I have no judgment.
Thou whoreson mandrake, thou art fitter to be worn
in my cap than to wait at my heels. I was never
manned with an agate till now: but I will inset you
neither in gold nor silver, but in vile apparel, and
send you back again to your master, for a jewel,--
the juvenal, the prince your master, whose chin is
not yet fledged. I will sooner have a beard grow in
the palm of my hand than he shall get one on his
cheek; and yet he will not stick to say his face is
a face-royal: God may finish it when he will, 'tis
not a hair amiss yet: he may keep it still at a
face-royal, for a barber shall never earn sixpence
out of it; and yet he'll be crowing as if he had
writ man ever since his father was a bachelor. He
may keep his own grace, but he's almost out of mine,
I can assure him. What said Master Dombledon about
the satin for my short cloak and my slops?

**Page**

He said, sir, you should procure him better
assurance than Bardolph: he would not take his
band and yours; he liked not the security.

**FALSTAFF**

Let him be damned, like the glutton! pray God his
tongue be hotter! A whoreson Achitophel! a rascally
yea-forsooth knave! to bear a gentleman in hand,
and then stand upon security! The whoreson

smooth-pates do now wear nothing but high shoes, and
bunches of keys at their girdles; and if a man is
through with them in honest taking up, then they
must stand upon security. I had as lief they would
put ratsbane in my mouth as offer to stop it with
security. I looked a' should have sent me two and
twenty yards of satin, as I am a true knight, and he
sends me security. Well, he may sleep in security;
for he hath the horn of abundance, and the lightness
of his wife shines through it: and yet cannot he
see, though he have his own lanthorn to light him.
Where's Bardolph?

**Page**

He's gone into Smithfield to buy your worship a horse.

**FALSTAFF**

I bought him in Paul's, and he'll buy me a horse in
Smithfield: an I could get me but a wife in the
stews, I were manned, horsed, and wived.

*Enter the Lord Chief-Justice and Servant*

**Page**

Sir, here comes the nobleman that committed the
Prince for striking him about Bardolph.

**FALSTAFF**

Wait, close; I will not see him.
Lord Chief-Justice What's he that goes there?

**Servant**

Falstaff, an't please your lordship.
Lord Chief-Justice He that was in question for the robbery?

**Servant**

He, my lord: but he hath since done good service at
Shrewsbury; and, as I hear, is now going with some
charge to the Lord John of Lancaster.
Lord Chief-Justice What, to York? Call him back again.

**Servant**

Sir John Falstaff!

**FALSTAFF**

Boy, tell him I am deaf.

**Page**

You must speak louder; my master is deaf.
Lord Chief-Justice I am sure he is, to the hearing of any thing good.
Go, pluck him by the elbow; I must speak with him.

**Servant**

Sir John!

**FALSTAFF**

What! a young knave, and begging! Is there not
wars? is there not employment? doth not the king
lack subjects? do not the rebels need soldiers?
Though it be a shame to be on any side but one, it
is worse shame to beg than to be on the worst side,
were it worse than the name of rebellion can tell
how to make it.

**Servant**

You mistake me, sir.

**FALSTAFF**

Why, sir, did I say you were an honest man? setting
my knighthood and my soldiership aside, I had lied
in my throat, if I had said so.

**Servant**

I pray you, sir, then set your knighthood and our
soldiership aside; and give me leave to tell you,
you lie in your throat, if you say I am any other
than an honest man.

**FALSTAFF**

I give thee leave to tell me so! I lay aside that
which grows to me! if thou gettest any leave of me,
hang me; if thou takest leave, thou wert better be
hanged. You hunt counter: hence! avaunt!
**Servant**
Sir, my lord would speak with you.
Lord Chief-Justice Sir John Falstaff, a word with you.
**FALSTAFF**
My good lord! God give your lordship good time of
day. I am glad to see your lordship abroad: I heard
say your lordship was sick: I hope your lordship
goes abroad by advice. Your lordship, though not
clean past your youth, hath yet some smack of age in
you, some relish of the saltness of time; and I must
humbly beseech your lordship to have a reverent care
of your health.
Lord Chief-Justice Sir John, I sent for you before your expedition to
Shrewsbury.
**FALSTAFF**
An't please your lordship, I hear his majesty is
returned with some discomfort from Wales.
Lord Chief-Justice I talk not of his majesty: you would not come when
I sent for you.
**FALSTAFF**
And I hear, moreover, his highness is fallen into
this same whoreson apoplexy.
Lord Chief-Justice Well, God mend him! I pray you, let me speak with
you.
**FALSTAFF**
This apoplexy is, as I take it, a kind of lethargy,
an't please your lordship; a kind of sleeping in the
blood, a whoreson tingling.
Lord Chief-Justice What tell you me of it? be it as it is.
**FALSTAFF**
It hath its original from much grief, from study and
perturbation of the brain: I have read the cause of
his effects in Galen: it is a kind of deafness.
Lord Chief-Justice I think you are fallen into the disease; for you
hear not what I say to you.
**FALSTAFF**
Very well, my lord, very well: rather, an't please
you, it is the disease of not listening, the malady
of not marking, that I am troubled withal.
Lord Chief-Justice To punish you by the heels would amend the
attention of your ears; and I care not if I do
become your physician.
**FALSTAFF**
I am as poor as Job, my lord, but not so patient:
your lordship may minister the potion of
imprisonment to me in respect of poverty; but how
should I be your patient to follow your
prescriptions, the wise may make some dram of a
scruple, or indeed a scruple itself.
Lord Chief-Justice I sent for you, when there were matters against you
for your life, to come speak with me.
**FALSTAFF**
As I was then advised by my learned counsel in the
laws of this land-service, I did not come.
Lord Chief-Justice Well, the truth is, Sir John, you live in great infamy.
**FALSTAFF**
He that buckles him in my belt cannot live in less.
Lord Chief-Justice Your means are very slender, and your waste is great.
**FALSTAFF**

I would it were otherwise; I would my means were
greater, and my waist slenderer.
Lord Chief-Justice You have misled the youthful prince.
**FALSTAFF**
The young prince hath misled me: I am the fellow
with the great belly, and he my dog.
Lord Chief-Justice Well, I am loath to gall a new-healed wound: your
day's service at Shrewsbury hath a little gilded
over your night's exploit on Gad's-hill: you may
thank the unquiet time for your quiet o'er-posting
that action.
**FALSTAFF**
My lord?
Lord Chief-Justice But since all is well, keep it so: wake not a
sleeping wolf.
**FALSTAFF**
To wake a wolf is as bad as to smell a fox.
Lord Chief-Justice What! you are as a candle, the better part burnt
out.
**FALSTAFF**
A wassail candle, my lord, all tallow: if I did say
of wax, my growth would approve the truth.
Lord Chief-Justice There is not a white hair on your face but should
have his effect of gravity.
**FALSTAFF**
His effect of gravy, gravy, gravy.
Lord Chief-Justice You follow the young prince up and down, like his
ill angel.
**FALSTAFF**
Not so, my lord; your ill angel is light; but I hope
he that looks upon me will take me without weighing:
and yet, in some respects, I grant, I cannot go: I
cannot tell. Virtue is of so little regard in these
costermonger times that true valour is turned
bear-herd: pregnancy is made a tapster, and hath
his quick wit wasted in giving reckonings: all the
other gifts appertinent to man, as the malice of
this age shapes them, are not worth a gooseberry.
You that are old consider not the capacities of us
that are young; you do measure the heat of our
livers with the bitterness of your galls: and we
that are in the vaward of our youth, I must confess,
are wags too.
Lord Chief-Justice Do you set down your name in the scroll of youth,
that are written down old with all the characters of
age? Have you not a moist eye? a dry hand? a
yellow cheek? a white beard? a decreasing leg? an
increasing belly? is not your voice broken? your
wind short? your chin double? your wit single? and
every part about you blasted with antiquity? and
will you yet call yourself young? Fie, fie, fie, Sir John!
**FALSTAFF**
My lord, I was born about three of the clock in the
afternoon, with a white head and something a round
belly. For my voice, I have lost it with halloing
and singing of anthems. To approve my youth
further, I will not: the truth is, I am only old in
judgment and understanding; and he that will caper
with me for a thousand marks, let him lend me the
money, and have at him! For the box of the ear that
the prince gave you, he gave it like a rude prince,
and you took it like a sensible lord. I have
chequed him for it, and the young lion repents;

marry, not in ashes and sackcloth, but in new silk
and old sack.
Lord Chief-Justice Well, God send the prince a better companion!
**FALSTAFF**
God send the companion a better prince! I cannot
rid my hands of him.
Lord Chief-Justice Well, the king hath severed you and Prince Harry: I
hear you are going with Lord John of Lancaster
against the Archbishop and the Earl of
Northumberland.
**FALSTAFF**
Yea; I thank your pretty sweet wit for it. But look
you pray, all you that kiss my lady Peace at home,
that our armies join not in a hot day; for, by the
Lord, I take but two shirts out with me, and I mean
not to sweat extraordinarily: if it be a hot day,
and I brandish any thing but a bottle, I would I
might never spit white again. There is not a
dangerous action can peep out his head but I am
thrust upon it: well, I cannot last ever: but it
was alway yet the trick of our English nation, if
they have a good thing, to make it too common. If
ye will needs say I am an old man, you should give
me rest. I would to God my name were not so
terrible to the enemy as it is: I were better to be
eaten to death with a rust than to be scoured to
nothing with perpetual motion.
Lord Chief-Justice Well, be honest, be honest; and God bless your
expedition!
**FALSTAFF**
Will your lordship lend me a thousand pound to
furnish me forth?
Lord Chief-Justice Not a penny, not a penny; you are too impatient to
bear crosses. Fare you well: commend me to my
cousin Westmoreland.
*Exeunt Chief-Justice and Servant*
**FALSTAFF**
If I do, fillip me with a three-man beetle. A man
can no more separate age and covetousness than a'
can part young limbs and lechery: but the gout
galls the one, and the pox pinches the other; and
so both the degrees prevent my curses. Boy!
**Page**
Sir?
**FALSTAFF**
What money is in my purse?
**Page**
Seven groats and two pence.
**FALSTAFF**
I can get no remedy against this consumption of the
purse: borrowing only lingers and lingers it out,
but the disease is incurable. Go bear this letter
to my Lord of Lancaster; this to the prince; this
to the Earl of Westmoreland; and this to old
Mistress Ursula, whom I have weekly sworn to marry
since I perceived the first white hair on my chin.
About it: you know where to find me.
*Exit Page*
A pox of this gout! or, a gout of this pox! for
the one or the other plays the rogue with my great
toe. 'Tis no matter if I do halt; I have the wars
for my colour, and my pension shall seem the more

reasonable. A good wit will make use of any thing:
I will turn diseases to commodity.
*Exit*
**SCENE III. York. The Archbishop's palace.**
*Enter the ARCHBISHOP OF YORK, the Lords HASTINGS, MOWBRAY, and BARDOLPH*
**ARCHBISHOP OF YORK**
Thus have you heard our cause and known our means;
And, my most noble friends, I pray you all,
Speak plainly your opinions of our hopes:
And first, lord marshal, what say you to it?
**MOWBRAY**
I well allow the occasion of our arms;
But gladly would be better satisfied
How in our means we should advance ourselves
To look with forehead bold and big enough
Upon the power and puissance of the king.
**HASTINGS**
Our present musters grow upon the file
To five and twenty thousand men of choice;
And our supplies live largely in the hope
Of great Northumberland, whose bosom burns
With an incensed fire of injuries.
**LORD BARDOLPH**
The question then, Lord Hastings, standeth thus;
Whether our present five and twenty thousand
May hold up head without Northumberland?
**HASTINGS**
With him, we may.
**LORD BARDOLPH**
Yea, marry, there's the point:
But if without him we be thought too feeble,
My judgment is, we should not step too far
Till we had his assistance by the hand;
For in a theme so bloody-faced as this
Conjecture, expectation, and surmise
Of aids incertain should not be admitted.
**ARCHBISHOP OF YORK**
'Tis very true, Lord Bardolph; for indeed
It was young Hotspur's case at Shrewsbury.
**LORD BARDOLPH**
It was, my lord; who lined himself with hope,
Eating the air on promise of supply,
Flattering himself in project of a power
Much smaller than the smallest of his thoughts:
And so, with great imagination
Proper to madmen, led his powers to death
And winking leap'd into destruction.
**HASTINGS**
But, by your leave, it never yet did hurt
To lay down likelihoods and forms of hope.
**LORD BARDOLPH**
Yes, if this present quality of war,
Indeed the instant action: a cause on foot
Lives so in hope as in an early spring
We see the appearing buds; which to prove fruit,
Hope gives not so much warrant as despair
That frosts will bite them. When we mean to build,
We first survey the plot, then draw the model;
And when we see the figure of the house,
Then must we rate the cost of the erection;
Which if we find outweighs ability,
What do we then but draw anew the model
In fewer offices, or at last desist

To build at all? Much more, in this great work,
Which is almost to pluck a kingdom down
And set another up, should we survey
The plot of situation and the model,
Consent upon a sure foundation,
Question surveyors, know our own estate,
How able such a work to undergo,
To weigh against his opposite; or else
We fortify in paper and in figures,
Using the names of men instead of men:
Like one that draws the model of a house
Beyond his power to build it; who, half through,
Gives o'er and leaves his part-created cost
A naked subject to the weeping clouds
And waste for churlish winter's tyranny.

**HASTINGS**

Grant that our hopes, yet likely of fair birth,
Should be still-born, and that we now possess'd
The utmost man of expectation,
I think we are a body strong enough,
Even as we are, to equal with the king.

**LORD BARDOLPH**

What, is the king but five and twenty thousand?

**HASTINGS**

To us no more; nay, not so much, Lord Bardolph.
For his divisions, as the times do brawl,
Are in three heads: one power against the French,
And one against Glendower; perforce a third
Must take up us: so is the unfirm king
In three divided; and his coffers sound
With hollow poverty and emptiness.

**ARCHBISHOP OF YORK**

That he should draw his several strengths together
And come against us in full puissance,
Need not be dreaded.

**HASTINGS**

If he should do so,
He leaves his back unarm'd, the French and Welsh
Baying him at the heels: never fear that.

**LORD BARDOLPH**

Who is it like should lead his forces hither?

**HASTINGS**

The Duke of Lancaster and Westmoreland;
Against the Welsh, himself and Harry Monmouth:
But who is substituted 'gainst the French,
I have no certain notice.

**ARCHBISHOP OF YORK**

Let us on,
And publish the occasion of our arms.
The commonwealth is sick of their own choice;
Their over-greedy love hath surfeited:
An habitation giddy and unsure
Hath he that buildeth on the vulgar heart.
O thou fond many, with what loud applause
Didst thou beat heaven with blessing Bolingbroke,
Before he was what thou wouldst have him be!
And being now trimm'd in thine own desires,
Thou, beastly feeder, art so full of him,
That thou provokest thyself to cast him up.
So, so, thou common dog, didst thou disgorge
Thy glutton bosom of the royal Richard;
And now thou wouldst eat thy dead vomit up,
And howl'st to find it. What trust is in

these times?
They that, when Richard lived, would have him die,
Are now become enamour'd on his grave:
Thou, that threw'st dust upon his goodly head
When through proud London he came sighing on
After the admired heels of Bolingbroke,
Criest now 'O earth, yield us that king again,
And take thou this!' O thoughts of men accursed!
Past and to come seems best; things present worst.
**MOWBRAY**
Shall we go draw our numbers and set on?
**HASTINGS**
We are time's subjects, and time bids be gone.
*Exeunt*

## ACT II

### SCENE I. London. A street.

*Enter MISTRESS QUICKLY, FANG and his Boy with her, and SNARE following.*

**MISTRESS QUICKLY**

Master Fang, have you entered the action?

**FANG**

It is entered.

**MISTRESS QUICKLY**

Where's your yeoman? Is't a lusty yeoman? will a'
stand to 't?

**FANG**

Sirrah, where's Snare?

**MISTRESS QUICKLY**

O Lord, ay! good Master Snare.

**SNARE**

Here, here.

**FANG**

Snare, we must arrest Sir John Falstaff.

**MISTRESS QUICKLY**

Yea, good Master Snare; I have entered him and all.

**SNARE**

It may chance cost some of us our lives, for he will stab.

**MISTRESS QUICKLY**

Alas the day! take heed of him; he stabbed me in
mine own house, and that most beastly: in good
faith, he cares not what mischief he does. If his
weapon be out: he will foin like any devil; he will
spare neither man, woman, nor child.

**FANG**

If I can close with him, I care not for his thrust.

**MISTRESS QUICKLY**

No, nor I neither: I'll be at your elbow.

**FANG**

An I but fist him once; an a' come but within my vice,--

**MISTRESS QUICKLY**

I am undone by his going; I warrant you, he's an
infinitive thing upon my score. Good Master Fang,
hold him sure: good Master Snare, let him not
'scape. A' comes continuantly to Pie-corner--saving
your manhoods--to buy a saddle; and he is indited to
dinner to the Lubber's-head in Lumbert street, to
Master Smooth's the silkman: I pray ye, since my
exion is entered and my case so openly known to the
world, let him be brought in to his answer. A
hundred mark is a long one for a poor lone woman to
bear: and I have borne, and borne, and borne, and
have been fubbed off, and fubbed off, and fubbed
off, from this day to that day, that it is a shame
to be thought on. There is no honesty in such
dealing; unless a woman should be made an ass and a
beast, to bear every knave's wrong. Yonder he
comes; and that errant malmsey-nose knave, Bardolph,
with him. Do your offices, do your offices: Master
Fang and Master Snare, do me, do me, do me your offices.

*Enter FALSTAFF, Page, and BARDOLPH*

**FALSTAFF**

How now! whose mare's dead? what's the matter?

**FANG**

Sir John, I arrest you at the suit of Mistress Quickly.

**FALSTAFF**

Away, varlets! Draw, Bardolph: cut me off the
villain's head: throw the quean in the channel.

**MISTRESS QUICKLY**

Throw me in the channel! I'll throw thee in the
channel. Wilt thou? wilt thou? thou bastardly
rogue! Murder, murder! Ah, thou honeysuckle
villain! wilt thou kill God's officers and the
king's? Ah, thou honey-seed rogue! thou art a
honey-seed, a man-queller, and a woman-queller.

**FALSTAFF**

Keep them off, Bardolph.

**FANG**

A rescue! a rescue!

**MISTRESS QUICKLY**

Good people, bring a rescue or two. Thou wo't, wo't
thou? Thou wo't, wo't ta? do, do, thou rogue! do,
thou hemp-seed!

**FALSTAFF**

Away, you scullion! you rampallion! You
fustilarian! I'll tickle your catastrophe.

*Enter the Lord Chief-Justice, and his men*

Lord Chief-Justice What is the matter? keep the peace here, ho!

**MISTRESS QUICKLY**

Good my lord, be good to me. I beseech you, stand to me.

Lord Chief-Justice How now, Sir John! what are you brawling here?
Doth this become your place, your time and business?
You should have been well on your way to York.
Stand from him, fellow: wherefore hang'st upon him?

**MISTRESS QUICKLY**

O most worshipful lord, an't please your grace, I am
a poor widow of Eastcheap, and he is arrested at my suit.

Lord Chief-Justice For what sum?

**MISTRESS QUICKLY**

It is more than for some, my lord; it is for all,
all I have. He hath eaten me out of house and home;
he hath put all my substance into that fat belly of
his: but I will have some of it out again, or I
will ride thee o' nights like the mare.

**FALSTAFF**

I think I am as like to ride the mare, if I have
any vantage of ground to get up.

Lord Chief-Justice How comes this, Sir John? Fie! what man of good
temper would endure this tempest of exclamation?
Are you not ashamed to enforce a poor widow to so
rough a course to come by her own?

**FALSTAFF**

What is the gross sum that I owe thee?

**MISTRESS QUICKLY**

Marry, if thou wert an honest man, thyself and the
money too. Thou didst swear to me upon a
parcel-gilt goblet, sitting in my Dolphin-chamber,
at the round table, by a sea-coal fire, upon
Wednesday in Wheeson week, when the prince broke
thy head for liking his father to a singing-man of
Windsor, thou didst swear to me then, as I was
washing thy wound, to marry me and make me my lady
thy wife. Canst thou deny it? Did not goodwife
Keech, the butcher's wife, come in then and call me
gossip Quickly? coming in to borrow a mess of
vinegar; telling us she had a good dish of prawns;
whereby thou didst desire to eat some; whereby I
told thee they were ill for a green wound? And
didst thou not, when she was gone down stairs,
desire me to be no more so familiarity with such
poor people; saying that ere long they should call
me madam? And didst thou not kiss me and bid me

fetch thee thirty shillings? I put thee now to thy
book-oath: deny it, if thou canst.
**FALSTAFF**
My lord, this is a poor mad soul; and she says up
and down the town that the eldest son is like you:
she hath been in good case, and the truth is,
poverty hath distracted her. But for these foolish
officers, I beseech you I may have redress against them.
Lord Chief-Justice Sir John, Sir John, I am well acquainted with your
manner of wrenching the true cause the false way. It
is not a confident brow, nor the throng of words
that come with such more than impudent sauciness
from you, can thrust me from a level consideration:
you have, as it appears to me, practised upon the
easy-yielding spirit of this woman, and made her
serve your uses both in purse and in person.
**MISTRESS QUICKLY**
Yea, in truth, my lord.
Lord Chief-Justice Pray thee, peace. Pay her the debt you owe her, and
unpay the villany you have done her: the one you
may do with sterling money, and the other with
current repentance.
**FALSTAFF**
My lord, I will not undergo this sneap without
reply. You call honourable boldness impudent
sauciness: if a man will make courtesy and say
nothing, he is virtuous: no, my lord, my humble
duty remembered, I will not be your suitor. I say
to you, I do desire deliverance from these officers,
being upon hasty employment in the king's affairs.
Lord Chief-Justice You speak as having power to do wrong: but answer
in the effect of your reputation, and satisfy this
poor woman.
**FALSTAFF**
Come hither, hostess.
*Enter GOWER*
Lord Chief-Justice Now, Master Gower, what news?
**GOWER**
The king, my lord, and Harry Prince of Wales
Are near at hand: the rest the paper tells.
**FALSTAFF**
As I am a gentleman.
**MISTRESS QUICKLY**
Faith, you said so before.
**FALSTAFF**
As I am a gentleman. Come, no more words of it.
**MISTRESS QUICKLY**
By this heavenly ground I tread on, I must be fain
to pawn both my plate and the tapestry of my
dining-chambers.
**FALSTAFF**
Glasses, glasses is the only drinking: and for thy
walls, a pretty slight drollery, or the story of
the Prodigal, or the German hunting in water-work,
is worth a thousand of these bed-hangings and these
fly-bitten tapestries. Let it be ten pound, if thou
canst. Come, an 'twere not for thy humours, there's
not a better wench in England. Go, wash thy face,
and draw the action. Come, thou must not be in
this humour with me; dost not know me? come, come, I
know thou wast set on to this.
**MISTRESS QUICKLY**

Pray thee, Sir John, let it be but twenty nobles: i'
faith, I am loath to pawn my plate, so God save me,
la!
**FALSTAFF**
Let it alone; I'll make other shift: you'll be a
fool still.
**MISTRESS QUICKLY**
Well, you shall have it, though I pawn my gown. I
hope you'll come to supper. You'll pay me all together?
**FALSTAFF**
Will I live?
*To BARDOLPH*
Go, with her, with her; hook on, hook on.
**MISTRESS QUICKLY**
Will you have Doll Tearsheet meet you at supper?
**FALSTAFF**
No more words; let's have her.
*Exeunt MISTRESS QUICKLY, BARDOLPH, Officers and Boy*
Lord Chief-Justice I have heard better news.
**FALSTAFF**
What's the news, my lord?
Lord Chief-Justice Where lay the king last night?
**GOWER**
At Basingstoke, my lord.
**FALSTAFF**
I hope, my lord, all's well: what is the news, my lord?
Lord Chief-Justice Come all his forces back?
**GOWER**
No; fifteen hundred foot, five hundred horse,
Are marched up to my lord of Lancaster,
Against Northumberland and the Archbishop.
**FALSTAFF**
Comes the king back from Wales, my noble lord?
Lord Chief-Justice You shall have letters of me presently:
Come, go along with me, good Master Gower.
**FALSTAFF**
My lord!
Lord Chief-Justice What's the matter?
**FALSTAFF**
Master Gower, shall I entreat you with me to dinner?
**GOWER**
I must wait upon my good lord here; I thank you,
good Sir John.
Lord Chief-Justice Sir John, you loiter here too long, being you are to
take soldiers up in counties as you go.
**FALSTAFF**
Will you sup with me, Master Gower?
Lord Chief-Justice What foolish master taught you these manners, Sir John?
**FALSTAFF**
Master Gower, if they become me not, he was a fool
that taught them me. This is the right fencing
grace, my lord; tap for tap, and so part fair.
Lord Chief-Justice Now the Lord lighten thee! thou art a great fool.
*Exeunt*
**SCENE II. London. Another street.**
*Enter PRINCE HENRY and POINS*
**PRINCE HENRY**
Before God, I am exceeding weary.
**POINS**
Is't come to that? I had thought weariness durst not
have attached one of so high blood.
**PRINCE HENRY**

Faith, it does me; though it discolours the
complexion of my greatness to acknowledge it. Doth
it not show vilely in me to desire small beer?
**POINS**
Why, a prince should not be so loosely studied as
to remember so weak a composition.
**PRINCE HENRY**
Belike then my appetite was not princely got; for,
by my troth, I do now remember the poor creature,
small beer. But, indeed, these humble
considerations make me out of love with my
greatness. What a disgrace is it to me to remember
thy name! or to know thy face to-morrow! or to
take note how many pair of silk stockings thou
hast, viz. these, and those that were thy
peach-coloured ones! or to bear the inventory of thy
shirts, as, one for superfluity, and another for
use! But that the tennis-court-keeper knows better
than I; for it is a low ebb of linen with thee when
thou keepest not racket there; as thou hast not done
a great while, because the rest of thy low
countries have made a shift to eat up thy holland:
and God knows, whether those that bawl out the ruins
of thy linen shall inherit his kingdom: but the
midwives say the children are not in the fault;
whereupon the world increases, and kindreds are
mightily strengthened.
**POINS**
How ill it follows, after you have laboured so hard,
you should talk so idly! Tell me, how many good
young princes would do so, their fathers being so
sick as yours at this time is?
**PRINCE HENRY**
Shall I tell thee one thing, Poins?
**POINS**
Yes, faith; and let it be an excellent good thing.
**PRINCE HENRY**
It shall serve among wits of no higher breeding than thine.
**POINS**
Go to; I stand the push of your one thing that you
will tell.
**PRINCE HENRY**
Marry, I tell thee, it is not meet that I should be
sad, now my father is sick: albeit I could tell
thee, as to one it pleases me, for fault of a
better, to call my friend, I could be sad, and sad
indeed too.
**POINS**
Very hardly upon such a subject.
**PRINCE HENRY**
By this hand thou thinkest me as far in the devil's
book as thou and Falstaff for obduracy and
persistency: let the end try the man. But I tell
thee, my heart bleeds inwardly that my father is so
sick: and keeping such vile company as thou art
hath in reason taken from me all ostentation of sorrow.
**POINS**
The reason?
**PRINCE HENRY**
What wouldst thou think of me, if I should weep?
**POINS**
I would think thee a most princely hypocrite.
**PRINCE HENRY**

It would be every man's thought; and thou art a
blessed fellow to think as every man thinks: never
a man's thought in the world keeps the road-way
better than thine: every man would think me an
hypocrite indeed. And what accites your most
worshipful thought to think so?

**POINS**

Why, because you have been so lewd and so much
engraffed to Falstaff.

**PRINCE HENRY**

And to thee.

**POINS**

By this light, I am well spoke on; I can hear it
with my own ears: the worst that they can say of
me is that I am a second brother and that I am a
proper fellow of my hands; and those two things, I
confess, I cannot help. By the mass, here comes Bardolph.

*Enter BARDOLPH and Page*

**PRINCE HENRY**

And the boy that I gave Falstaff: a' had him from
me Christian; and look, if the fat villain have not
transformed him ape.

**BARDOLPH**

God save your grace!

**PRINCE HENRY**

And yours, most noble Bardolph!

**BARDOLPH**

Come, you virtuous ass, you bashful fool, must you
be blushing? wherefore blush you now? What a
maidenly man-at-arms are you become! Is't such a
matter to get a pottle-pot's maidenhead?

**Page**

A' calls me e'en now, my lord, through a red
lattice, and I could discern no part of his face
from the window: at last I spied his eyes, and
methought he had made two holes in the ale-wife's
new petticoat and so peeped through.

**PRINCE HENRY**

Has not the boy profited?

**BARDOLPH**

Away, you whoreson upright rabbit, away!

**Page**

Away, you rascally Althaea's dream, away!

**PRINCE HENRY**

Instruct us, boy; what dream, boy?

**Page**

Marry, my lord, Althaea dreamed she was delivered
of a fire-brand; and therefore I call him her dream.

**PRINCE HENRY**

A crown's worth of good interpretation: there 'tis,
boy.

**POINS**

O, that this good blossom could be kept from
cankers! Well, there is sixpence to preserve thee.

**BARDOLPH**

An you do not make him hanged among you, the
gallows shall have wrong.

**PRINCE HENRY**

And how doth thy master, Bardolph?

**BARDOLPH**

Well, my lord. He heard of your grace's coming to
town: there's a letter for you.

**POINS**

Delivered with good respect. And how doth the
martlemas, your master?
**BARDOLPH**
In bodily health, sir.
**POINS**
Marry, the immortal part needs a physician; but
that moves not him: though that be sick, it dies
not.
**PRINCE HENRY**
I do allow this wen to be as familiar with me as my
dog; and he holds his place; for look you how be writes.
**POINS**
|Reads| 'John Falstaff, knight,'--every man must
know that, as oft as he has occasion to name
himself: even like those that are kin to the king;
for they never prick their finger but they say,
'There's some of the king's blood spilt.' 'How
comes that?' says he, that takes upon him not to
conceive. The answer is as ready as a borrower's
cap, 'I am the king's poor cousin, sir.'
**PRINCE HENRY**
Nay, they will be kin to us, or they will fetch it
from Japhet. But to the letter.
**POINS**
|Reads| 'Sir John Falstaff, knight, to the son of
the king, nearest his father, Harry Prince of
Wales, greeting.' Why, this is a certificate.
**PRINCE HENRY**
Peace!
**POINS**
|Reads| 'I will imitate the honourable Romans in
brevity:' he sure means brevity in breath,
short-winded. 'I commend me to thee, I commend
thee, and I leave thee. Be not too familiar with
Poins; for he misuses thy favours so much, that he
swears thou art to marry his sister Nell. Repent
at idle times as thou mayest; and so, farewell.
Thine, by yea and no, which is as much as to
say, as thou usest him, JACK FALSTAFF with my
familiars, JOHN with my brothers and sisters,
and SIR JOHN with all Europe.'
My lord, I'll steep this letter in sack and make him eat it.
**PRINCE HENRY**
That's to make him eat twenty of his words. But do
you use me thus, Ned? must I marry your sister?
**POINS**
God send the wench no worse fortune! But I never said so.
**PRINCE HENRY**
Well, thus we play the fools with the time, and the
spirits of the wise sit in the clouds and mock us.
Is your master here in London?
**BARDOLPH**
Yea, my lord.
**PRINCE HENRY**
Where sups he? doth the old boar feed in the old frank?
**BARDOLPH**
At the old place, my lord, in Eastcheap.
**PRINCE HENRY**
What company?
**Page**
Ephesians, my lord, of the old church.
**PRINCE HENRY**
Sup any women with him?

**Page**
None, my lord, but old Mistress Quickly and
Mistress Doll Tearsheet.
**PRINCE HENRY**
What pagan may that be?
**Page**
A proper gentlewoman, sir, and a kinswoman of my master's.
**PRINCE HENRY**
Even such kin as the parish heifers are to the town
bull. Shall we steal upon them, Ned, at supper?
**POINS**
I am your shadow, my lord; I'll follow you.
**PRINCE HENRY**
Sirrah, you boy, and Bardolph, no word to your
master that I am yet come to town: there's for
your silence.
**BARDOLPH**
I have no tongue, sir.
**Page**
And for mine, sir, I will govern it.
**PRINCE HENRY**
Fare you well; go.
*Exeunt BARDOLPH and Page*
This Doll Tearsheet should be some road.
**POINS**
I warrant you, as common as the way between Saint
Alban's and London.
**PRINCE HENRY**
How might we see Falstaff bestow himself to-night
in his true colours, and not ourselves be seen?
**POINS**
Put on two leathern jerkins and aprons, and wait
upon him at his table as drawers.
**PRINCE HENRY**
From a God to a bull? a heavy decension! it was
Jove's case. From a prince to a prentice? a low
transformation! that shall be mine; for in every
thing the purpose must weigh with the folly.
Follow me, Ned.
*Exeunt*
**SCENE III. Warkworth. Before the castle.**
*Enter NORTHUMBERLAND, LADY NORTHUMBERLAND, and LADY PERCY*
**NORTHUMBERLAND**
I pray thee, loving wife, and gentle daughter,
Give even way unto my rough affairs:
Put not you on the visage of the times
And be like them to Percy troublesome.
LADY
**NORTHUMBERLAND**
I have given over, I will speak no more:
Do what you will; your wisdom be your guide.
**NORTHUMBERLAND**
Alas, sweet wife, my honour is at pawn;
And, but my going, nothing can redeem it.
**LADY PERCY**
O yet, for God's sake, go not to these wars!
The time was, father, that you broke your word,
When you were more endeared to it than now;
When your own Percy, when my heart's dear Harry,
Threw many a northward look to see his father
Bring up his powers; but he did long in vain.
Who then persuaded you to stay at home?
There were two honours lost, yours and your son's.

For yours, the God of heaven brighten it!
For his, it stuck upon him as the sun
In the grey vault of heaven, and by his light
Did all the chivalry of England move
To do brave acts: he was indeed the glass
Wherein the noble youth did dress themselves:
He had no legs that practised not his gait;
And speaking thick, which nature made his blemish,
Became the accents of the valiant;
For those that could speak low and tardily
Would turn their own perfection to abuse,
To seem like him: so that in speech, in gait,
In diet, in affections of delight,
In military rules, humours of blood,
He was the mark and glass, copy and book,
That fashion'd others. And him, O wondrous him!
O miracle of men! him did you leave,
Second to none, unseconded by you,
To look upon the hideous god of war
In disadvantage; to abide a field
Where nothing but the sound of Hotspur's name
Did seem defensible: so you left him.
Never, O never, do his ghost the wrong
To hold your honour more precise and nice
With others than with him! let them alone:
The marshal and the archbishop are strong:
Had my sweet Harry had but half their numbers,
To-day might I, hanging on Hotspur's neck,
Have talk'd of Monmouth's grave.
**NORTHUMBERLAND**
Beshrew your heart,
Fair daughter, you do draw my spirits from me
With new lamenting ancient oversights.
But I must go and meet with danger there,
Or it will seek me in another place
And find me worse provided.
LADY
**NORTHUMBERLAND**
O, fly to Scotland,
Till that the nobles and the armed commons
Have of their puissance made a little taste.
**LADY PERCY**
If they get ground and vantage of the king,
Then join you with them, like a rib of steel,
To make strength stronger; but, for all our loves,
First let them try themselves. So did your son;
He was so suffer'd: so came I a widow;
And never shall have length of life enough
To rain upon remembrance with mine eyes,
That it may grow and sprout as high as heaven,
For recordation to my noble husband.
**NORTHUMBERLAND**
Come, come, go in with me. 'Tis with my mind
As with the tide swell'd up unto his height,
That makes a still-stand, running neither way:
Fain would I go to meet the archbishop,
But many thousand reasons hold me back.
I will resolve for Scotland: there am I,
Till time and vantage crave my company.
*Exeunt*
**SCENE IV. London. The Boar's-head Tavern in Eastcheap.**
*Enter two Drawers*
**First Drawer**

What the devil hast thou brought there? apple-johns?
thou knowest Sir John cannot endure an apple-john.
**Second Drawer**
Mass, thou sayest true. The prince once set a dish
of apple-johns before him, and told him there were
five more Sir Johns, and, putting off his hat, said
'I will now take my leave of these six dry, round,
old, withered knights.' It angered him to the
heart: but he hath forgot that.
**First Drawer**
Why, then, cover, and set them down: and see if
thou canst find out Sneak's noise; Mistress
Tearsheet would fain hear some music. Dispatch: the
room where they supped is too hot; they'll come in straight.
**Second Drawer**
Sirrah, here will be the prince and Master Poins
anon; and they will put on two of our jerkins and
aprons; and Sir John must not know of it: Bardolph
hath brought word.
**First Drawer**
By the mass, here will be old Utis: it will be an
excellent stratagem.
**Second Drawer**
I'll see if I can find out Sneak.
*Exit*
*Enter MISTRESS QUICKLY and DOLL TEARSHEET*
**MISTRESS QUICKLY**
I' faith, sweetheart, methinks now you are in an
excellent good temperality: your pulsidge beats as
extraordinarily as heart would desire; and your
colour, I warrant you, is as red as any rose, in good
truth, la! But, i' faith, you have drunk too much
canaries; and that's a marvellous searching wine,
and it perfumes the blood ere one can say 'What's
this?' How do you now?
**DOLL TEARSHEET**
Better than I was: hem!
**MISTRESS QUICKLY**
Why, that's well said; a good heart's worth gold.
Lo, here comes Sir John.
*Enter FALSTAFF*
**FALSTAFF**
[Singing] 'When Arthur first in court,'
--Empty the jordan.
*Exit First Drawer*
*Singing*
--'And was a worthy king.' How now, Mistress Doll!
**MISTRESS QUICKLY**
Sick of a calm; yea, good faith.
**FALSTAFF**
So is all her sect; an they be once in a calm, they are sick.
**DOLL TEARSHEET**
You muddy rascal, is that all the comfort you give me?
**FALSTAFF**
You make fat rascals, Mistress Doll.
**DOLL TEARSHEET**
I make them! gluttony and diseases make them; I
make them not.
**FALSTAFF**
If the cook help to make the gluttony, you help to
make the diseases, Doll: we catch of you, Doll, we
catch of you; grant that, my poor virtue grant that.
**DOLL TEARSHEET**

Yea, joy, our chains and our jewels.
**FALSTAFF**
'Your broaches, pearls, and ouches:' for to serve bravely is to come halting off, you know: to come off the breach with his pike bent bravely, and to surgery bravely; to venture upon the charged chambers bravely,--
**DOLL TEARSHEET**
Hang yourself, you muddy conger, hang yourself!
**MISTRESS QUICKLY**
By my troth, this is the old fashion; you two never meet but you fall to some discord: you are both, i' good truth, as rheumatic as two dry toasts; you cannot one bear with another's confirmities. What the good-year! one must bear, and that must be you: you are the weaker vessel, as they say, the emptier vessel.
**DOLL TEARSHEET**
Can a weak empty vessel bear such a huge full hogshead? there's a whole merchant's venture of Bourdeaux stuff in him; you have not seen a hulk better stuffed in the hold. Come, I'll be friends with thee, Jack: thou art going to the wars; and whether I shall ever see thee again or no, there is nobody cares.
*Re-enter First Drawer*
**First Drawer**
Sir, Ancient Pistol's below, and would speak with you.
**DOLL TEARSHEET**
Hang him, swaggering rascal! let him not come hither: it is the foul-mouthed'st rogue in England.
**MISTRESS QUICKLY**
If he swagger, let him not come here: no, by my faith; I must live among my neighbours: I'll no swaggerers: I am in good name and fame with the very best: shut the door; there comes no swaggerers here: I have not lived all this while, to have swaggering now: shut the door, I pray you.
**FALSTAFF**
Dost thou hear, hostess?
**MISTRESS QUICKLY**
Pray ye, pacify yourself, Sir John: there comes no swaggerers here.
**FALSTAFF**
Dost thou hear? it is mine ancient.
**MISTRESS QUICKLY**
Tilly-fally, Sir John, ne'er tell me: your ancient swaggerer comes not in my doors. I was before Master Tisick, the debuty, t'other day; and, as he said to me, 'twas no longer ago than Wednesday last, 'I' good faith, neighbour Quickly,' says he; Master Dumbe, our minister, was by then; 'neighbour Quickly,' says he, 'receive those that are civil; for,' said he, 'you are in an ill name:' now a' said so, I can tell whereupon; 'for,' says he, 'you are an honest woman, and well thought on; therefore take heed what guests you receive: receive,' says he, 'no swaggering companions.' There comes none here: you would bless you to hear what he said: no, I'll no swaggerers.
**FALSTAFF**

He's no swaggerer, hostess; a tame cheater, i'
faith; you may stroke him as gently as a puppy
greyhound: he'll not swagger with a Barbary hen, if
her feathers turn back in any show of resistance.
Call him up, drawer.
*Exit First Drawer*
**MISTRESS QUICKLY**
Cheater, call you him? I will bar no honest man my
house, nor no cheater: but I do not love
swaggering, by my troth; I am the worse, when one
says swagger: feel, masters, how I shake; look you,
I warrant you.
**DOLL TEARSHEET**
So you do, hostess.
**MISTRESS QUICKLY**
Do I? yea, in very truth, do I, an 'twere an aspen
leaf: I cannot abide swaggerers.
*Enter PISTOL, BARDOLPH, and Page*
**PISTOL**
God save you, Sir John!
**FALSTAFF**
Welcome, Ancient Pistol. Here, Pistol, I charge
you with a cup of sack: do you discharge upon mine hostess.
**PISTOL**
I will discharge upon her, Sir John, with two bullets.
**FALSTAFF**
She is Pistol-proof, sir; you shall hardly offend
her.
**MISTRESS QUICKLY**
Come, I'll drink no proofs nor no bullets: I'll
drink no more than will do me good, for no man's
pleasure, I.
**PISTOL**
Then to you, Mistress Dorothy; I will charge you.
**DOLL TEARSHEET**
Charge me! I scorn you, scurvy companion. What!
you poor, base, rascally, cheating, lack-linen
mate! Away, you mouldy rogue, away! I am meat for
your master.
**PISTOL**
I know you, Mistress Dorothy.
**DOLL TEARSHEET**
Away, you cut-purse rascal! you filthy bung, away!
by this wine, I'll thrust my knife in your mouldy
chaps, an you play the saucy cuttle with me. Away,
you bottle-ale rascal! you basket-hilt stale
juggler, you! Since when, I pray you, sir? God's
light, with two points on your shoulder? much!
**PISTOL**
God let me not live, but I will murder your ruff for this.
**FALSTAFF**
No more, Pistol; I would not have you go off here:
discharge yourself of our company, Pistol.
**MISTRESS QUICKLY**
No, Good Captain Pistol; not here, sweet captain.
**DOLL TEARSHEET**
Captain! thou abominable damned cheater, art thou
not ashamed to be called captain? An captains were
of my mind, they would truncheon you out, for
taking their names upon you before you have earned
them. You a captain! you slave, for what? for
tearing a poor whore's ruff in a bawdy-house? He a
captain! hang him, rogue! he lives upon mouldy

stewed prunes and dried cakes. A captain! God's light, these villains will make the word as odious as the word 'occupy;' which was an excellent good word before it was ill sorted: therefore captains had need look to 't.

**BARDOLPH**

Pray thee, go down, good ancient.

**FALSTAFF**

Hark thee hither, Mistress Doll.

**PISTOL**

Not I I tell thee what, Corporal Bardolph, I could tear her: I'll be revenged of her.

**Page**

Pray thee, go down.

**PISTOL**

I'll see her damned first; to Pluto's damned lake, by this hand, to the infernal deep, with Erebus and tortures vile also. Hold hook and line, say I. Down, down, dogs! down, faitors! Have we not Hiren here?

**MISTRESS QUICKLY**

Good Captain Peesel, be quiet; 'tis very late, i' faith: I beseek you now, aggravate your choler.

**PISTOL**

These be good humours, indeed! Shall pack-horses
And hollow pamper'd jades of Asia,
Which cannot go but thirty mile a-day,
Compare with Caesars, and with Cannibals,
And Trojan Greeks? nay, rather damn them with
King Cerberus; and let the welkin roar.
Shall we fall foul for toys?

**MISTRESS QUICKLY**

By my troth, captain, these are very bitter words.

**BARDOLPH**

Be gone, good ancient: this will grow to abrawl anon.

**PISTOL**

Die men like dogs! give crowns like pins! Have we not Heren here?

**MISTRESS QUICKLY**

O' my word, captain, there's none such here. What the good-year! do you think I would deny her? For God's sake, be quiet.

**PISTOL**

Then feed, and be fat, my fair Calipolis.
Come, give's some sack.
'Si fortune me tormente, sperato me contento.'
Fear we broadsides? no, let the fiend give fire:
Give me some sack: and, sweetheart, lie thou there.
*Laying down his sword*
Come we to full points here; and are etceteras nothing?

**FALSTAFF**

Pistol, I would be quiet.

**PISTOL**

Sweet knight, I kiss thy neaf: what! we have seen the seven stars.

**DOLL TEARSHEET**

For God's sake, thrust him down stairs: I cannot endure such a fustian rascal.

**PISTOL**

Thrust him down stairs! know we not Galloway nags?

**FALSTAFF**

Quoit him down, Bardolph, like a shove-groat
shilling: nay, an a' do nothing but speak nothing,
a' shall be nothing here.

**BARDOLPH**

Come, get you down stairs.

**PISTOL**

What! shall we have incision? shall we imbrue?

*Snatching up his sword*

Then death rock me asleep, abridge my doleful days!
Why, then, let grievous, ghastly, gaping wounds
Untwine the Sisters Three! Come, Atropos, I say!

**MISTRESS QUICKLY**

Here's goodly stuff toward!

**FALSTAFF**

Give me my rapier, boy.

**DOLL TEARSHEET**

I pray thee, Jack, I pray thee, do not draw.

**FALSTAFF**

Get you down stairs.

*Drawing, and driving PISTOL out*

**MISTRESS QUICKLY**

Here's a goodly tumult! I'll forswear keeping
house, afore I'll be in these tirrits and frights.
So; murder, I warrant now. Alas, alas! put up
your naked weapons, put up your naked weapons.

*Exeunt PISTOL and BARDOLPH*

**DOLL TEARSHEET**

I pray thee, Jack, be quiet; the rascal's gone.
Ah, you whoreson little valiant villain, you!

**MISTRESS QUICKLY**

He you not hurt i' the groin? methought a' made a
shrewd thrust at your belly.

*Re-enter BARDOLPH*

**FALSTAFF**

Have you turned him out o' doors?

**BARDOLPH**

Yea, sir. The rascal's drunk: you have hurt him,
sir, i' the shoulder.

**FALSTAFF**

A rascal! to brave me!

**DOLL TEARSHEET**

Ah, you sweet little rogue, you! alas, poor ape,
how thou sweatest! come, let me wipe thy face;
come on, you whoreson chops: ah, rogue! i'faith, I
love thee: thou art as valorous as Hector of Troy,
worth five of Agamemnon, and ten times better than
the Nine Worthies: ah, villain!

**FALSTAFF**

A rascally slave! I will toss the rogue in a blanket.

**DOLL TEARSHEET**

Do, an thou darest for thy heart: an thou dost,
I'll canvass thee between a pair of sheets.

*Enter Music*

**Page**

The music is come, sir.

**FALSTAFF**

Let them play. Play, sirs. Sit on my knee, Doll.
A rascal bragging slave! the rogue fled from me
like quicksilver.

**DOLL TEARSHEET**

I' faith, and thou followedst him like a church.
Thou whoreson little tidy Bartholomew boar-pig,

when wilt thou leave fighting o' days and foining
o' nights, and begin to patch up thine old body for heaven?
*Enter, behind, PRINCE HENRY and POINS, disguised*
**FALSTAFF**
Peace, good Doll! do not speak like a death's-head;
do not bid me remember mine end.
**DOLL TEARSHEET**
Sirrah, what humour's the prince of?
**FALSTAFF**
A good shallow young fellow: a' would have made a
good pantler, a' would ha' chipp'd bread well.
**DOLL TEARSHEET**
They say Poins has a good wit.
**FALSTAFF**
He a good wit? hang him, baboon! his wit's as thick
as Tewksbury mustard; there's no more conceit in him
than is in a mallet.
**DOLL TEARSHEET**
Why does the prince love him so, then?
**FALSTAFF**
Because their legs are both of a bigness, and a'
plays at quoits well, and eats conger and fennel,
and drinks off candles' ends for flap-dragons, and
rides the wild-mare with the boys, and jumps upon
joined-stools, and swears with a good grace, and
wears his boots very smooth, like unto the sign of
the leg, and breeds no bate with telling of discreet
stories; and such other gambol faculties a' has,
that show a weak mind and an able body, for the
which the prince admits him: for the prince himself
is such another; the weight of a hair will turn the
scales between their avoirdupois.
**PRINCE HENRY**
Would not this nave of a wheel have his ears cut off?
**POINS**
Let's beat him before his whore.
**PRINCE HENRY**
Look, whether the withered elder hath not his poll
clawed like a parrot.
**POINS**
Is it not strange that desire should so many years
outlive performance?
**FALSTAFF**
Kiss me, Doll.
**PRINCE HENRY**
Saturn and Venus this year in conjunction! what
says the almanac to that?
**POINS**
And look, whether the fiery Trigon, his man, be not
lisping to his master's old tables, his note-book,
his counsel-keeper.
**FALSTAFF**
Thou dost give me flattering busses.
**DOLL TEARSHEET**
By my troth, I kiss thee with a most constant heart.
**FALSTAFF**
I am old, I am old.
**DOLL TEARSHEET**
I love thee better than I love e'er a scurvy young
boy of them all.
**FALSTAFF**
What stuff wilt have a kirtle of? I shall receive
money o' Thursday: shalt have a cap to-morrow. A

merry song, come: it grows late; we'll to bed.
Thou'lt forget me when I am gone.

**DOLL TEARSHEET**

By my troth, thou'lt set me a-weeping, an thou
sayest so: prove that ever I dress myself handsome
till thy return: well, harken at the end.

**FALSTAFF**

Some sack, Francis.

**PRINCE HENRY POINS**

Anon, anon, sir.

*Coming forward*

**FALSTAFF**

Ha! a bastard son of the king's? And art not thou
Poins his brother?

**PRINCE HENRY**

Why, thou globe of sinful continents! what a life
dost thou lead!

**FALSTAFF**

A better than thou: I am a gentleman; thou art a drawer.

**PRINCE HENRY**

Very true, sir; and I come to draw you out by the ears.

**MISTRESS QUICKLY**

O, the Lord preserve thy good grace! by my troth,
welcome to London. Now, the Lord bless that sweet
face of thine! O, Jesu, are you come from Wales?

**FALSTAFF**

Thou whoreson mad compound of majesty, by this light
flesh and corrupt blood, thou art welcome.

**DOLL TEARSHEET**

How, you fat fool! I scorn you.

**POINS**

My lord, he will drive you out of your revenge and
turn all to a merriment, if you take not the heat.

**PRINCE HENRY**

You whoreson candle-mine, you, how vilely did you
speak of me even now before this honest, virtuous,
civil gentlewoman!

**MISTRESS QUICKLY**

God's blessing of your good heart! and so she is,
by my troth.

**FALSTAFF**

Didst thou hear me?

**PRINCE HENRY**

Yea, and you knew me, as you did when you ran away
by Gad's-hill: you knew I was at your back, and
spoke it on purpose to try my patience.

**FALSTAFF**

No, no, no; not so; I did not think thou wast within hearing.

**PRINCE HENRY**

I shall drive you then to confess the wilful abuse;
and then I know how to handle you.

**FALSTAFF**

No abuse, Hal, o' mine honour, no abuse.

**PRINCE HENRY**

Not to dispraise me, and call me pantier and
bread-chipper and I know not what?

**FALSTAFF**

No abuse, Hal.

**POINS**

No abuse?

**FALSTAFF**

No abuse, Ned, i' the world; honest Ned, none. I
dispraised him before the wicked, that the wicked

might not fall in love with him; in which doing, I
have done the part of a careful friend and a true
subject, and thy father is to give me thanks for it.
No abuse, Hal: none, Ned, none: no, faith, boys, none.

**PRINCE HENRY**

See now, whether pure fear and entire cowardice doth
not make thee wrong this virtuous gentlewoman to
close with us? is she of the wicked? is thine
hostess here of the wicked? or is thy boy of the
wicked? or honest Bardolph, whose zeal burns in his
nose, of the wicked?

**POINS**

Answer, thou dead elm, answer.

**FALSTAFF**

The fiend hath pricked down Bardolph irrecoverable;
and his face is Lucifer's privy-kitchen, where he
doth nothing but roast malt-worms. For the boy,
there is a good angel about him; but the devil
outbids him too.

**PRINCE HENRY**

For the women?

**FALSTAFF**

For one of them, she is in hell already, and burns
poor souls. For the other, I owe her money, and
whether she be damned for that, I know not.

**MISTRESS QUICKLY**

No, I warrant you.

**FALSTAFF**

No, I think thou art not; I think thou art quit for
that. Marry, there is another indictment upon thee,
for suffering flesh to be eaten in thy house,
contrary to the law; for the which I think thou wilt howl.

**MISTRESS QUICKLY**

All victuallers do so; what's a joint of mutton or
two in a whole Lent?

**PRINCE HENRY**

You, gentlewoman,-

**DOLL TEARSHEET**

What says your grace?

**FALSTAFF**

His grace says that which his flesh rebels against.

*Knocking within*

**MISTRESS QUICKLY**

Who knocks so loud at door? Look to the door there, Francis.

*Enter PETO*

**PRINCE HENRY**

Peto, how now! what news?

**PETO**

The king your father is at Westminster:
And there are twenty weak and wearied posts
Come from the north: and, as I came along,
I met and overtook a dozen captains,
Bare-headed, sweating, knocking at the taverns,
And asking every one for Sir John Falstaff.

**PRINCE HENRY**

By heaven, Poins, I feel me much to blame,
So idly to profane the precious time,
When tempest of commotion, like the south
Borne with black vapour, doth begin to melt
And drop upon our bare unarmed heads.
Give me my sword and cloak. Falstaff, good night.

*Exeunt PRINCE HENRY, POINS, PETO and BARDOLPH*

**FALSTAFF**

Now comes in the sweetest morsel of the night, and
we must hence and leave it unpicked.
*Knocking within*
More knocking at the door!
*Re-enter BARDOLPH*
How now! what's the matter?
**BARDOLPH**
You must away to court, sir, presently;
A dozen captains stay at door for you.
**FALSTAFF**
[To the Page] Pay the musicians, sirrah. Farewell,
hostess; farewell, Doll. You see, my good wenches,
how men of merit are sought after: the undeserver
may sleep, when the man of action is called on.
Farewell good wenches: if I be not sent away post,
I will see you again ere I go.
**DOLL TEARSHEET**
I cannot speak; if my heart be not read to burst,--
well, sweet Jack, have a care of thyself.
**FALSTAFF**
Farewell, farewell.
*Exeunt FALSTAFF and BARDOLPH*
**MISTRESS QUICKLY**
Well, fare thee well: I have known thee these
twenty-nine years, come peascod-time; but an
honester and truer-hearted man,--well, fare thee well.
**BARDOLPH**
[Within] Mistress Tearsheet!
**MISTRESS QUICKLY**
What's the matter?
**BARDOLPH**
[Within] Good Mistress Tearsheet, come to my master.
**MISTRESS QUICKLY**
O, run, Doll, run; run, good Doll: come.
*She comes blubbered*
Yea, will you come, Doll?
*Exeunt*

**SCENE I. Westminster. The palace.**

*Enter KING HENRY IV in his nightgown, with a Page*

**KING HENRY IV**

Go call the Earls of Surrey and of Warwick;
But, ere they come, bid them o'er-read these letters,
And well consider of them; make good speed.

*Exit Page*

How many thousand of my poorest subjects
Are at this hour asleep! O sleep, O gentle sleep,
Nature's soft nurse, how have I frighted thee,
That thou no more wilt weigh my eyelids down
And steep my senses in forgetfulness?
Why rather, sleep, liest thou in smoky cribs,
Upon uneasy pallets stretching thee
And hush'd with buzzing night-flies to thy slumber,
Than in the perfumed chambers of the great,
Under the canopies of costly state,
And lull'd with sound of sweetest melody?
O thou dull god, why liest thou with the vile
In loathsome beds, and leavest the kingly couch
A watch-case or a common 'larum-bell?
Wilt thou upon the high and giddy mast
Seal up the ship-boy's eyes, and rock his brains
In cradle of the rude imperious surge
And in the visitation of the winds,
Who take the ruffian billows by the top,
Curling their monstrous heads and hanging them
With deafening clamour in the slippery clouds,
That, with the hurly, death itself awakes?
Canst thou, O partial sleep, give thy repose
To the wet sea-boy in an hour so rude,
And in the calmest and most stillest night,
With all appliances and means to boot,
Deny it to a king? Then happy low, lie down!
Uneasy lies the head that wears a crown.

*Enter WARWICK and SURREY*

**WARWICK**

Many good morrows to your majesty!

**KING HENRY IV**

Is it good morrow, lords?

**WARWICK**

'Tis one o'clock, and past.

**KING HENRY IV**

Why, then, good morrow to you all, my lords.
Have you read o'er the letters that I sent you?

**WARWICK**

We have, my liege.

**KING HENRY IV**

Then you perceive the body of our kingdom
How foul it is; what rank diseases grow
And with what danger, near the heart of it.

**WARWICK**

It is but as a body yet distemper'd;
Which to his former strength may be restored
With good advice and little medicine:
My Lord Northumberland will soon be cool'd.

**KING HENRY IV**

O God! that one might read the book of fate,
And see the revolution of the times
Make mountains level, and the continent,
Weary of solid firmness, melt itself
Into the sea! and, other times, to see

The beachy girdle of the ocean
Too wide for Neptune's hips; how chances mock,
And changes fill the cup of alteration
With divers liquors! O, if this were seen,
The happiest youth, viewing his progress through,
What perils past, what crosses to ensue,
Would shut the book, and sit him down and die.
'Tis not 'ten years gone
Since Richard and Northumberland, great friends,
Did feast together, and in two years after
Were they at wars: it is but eight years since
This Percy was the man nearest my soul,
Who like a brother toil'd in my affairs
And laid his love and life under my foot,
Yea, for my sake, even to the eyes of Richard
Gave him defiance. But which of you was by--
You, cousin Nevil, as I may remember--
*To WARWICK*
When Richard, with his eye brimful of tears,
Then cheque'd and rated by Northumberland,
Did speak these words, now proved a prophecy?
'Northumberland, thou ladder by the which
My cousin Bolingbroke ascends my throne;'
Though then, God knows, I had no such intent,
But that necessity so bow'd the state
That I and greatness were compell'd to kiss:
'The time shall come,' thus did he follow it,
'The time will come, that foul sin, gathering head,
Shall break into corruption:' so went on,
Foretelling this same time's condition
And the division of our amity.
**WARWICK**
There is a history in all men's lives,
Figuring the nature of the times deceased;
The which observed, a man may prophesy,
With a near aim, of the main chance of things
As yet not come to life, which in their seeds
And weak beginnings lie intreasured.
Such things become the hatch and brood of time;
And by the necessary form of this
King Richard might create a perfect guess
That great Northumberland, then false to him,
Would of that seed grow to a greater falseness;
Which should not find a ground to root upon,
Unless on you.
**KING HENRY IV**
Are these things then necessities?
Then let us meet them like necessities:
And that same word even now cries out on us:
They say the bishop and Northumberland
Are fifty thousand strong.
**WARWICK**
It cannot be, my lord;
Rumour doth double, like the voice and echo,
The numbers of the fear'd. Please it your grace
To go to bed. Upon my soul, my lord,
The powers that you already have sent forth
Shall bring this prize in very easily.
To comfort you the more, I have received
A certain instance that Glendower is dead.
Your majesty hath been this fortnight ill,
And these unseason'd hours perforce must add
Unto your sickness.

**KING HENRY IV**
I will take your counsel:
And were these inward wars once out of hand,
We would, dear lords, unto the Holy Land.
*Exeunt*
**SCENE II. Gloucestershire. Before SHALLOW'S house.**
*Enter SHALLOW and SILENCE, meeting; MOULDY, SHADOW, WART, FEEBLE, BULLCALF, a Servant or two with them*
**SHALLOW**
Come on, come on, come on, sir; give me your hand,
sir, give me your hand, sir: an early stirrer, by
the rood! And how doth my good cousin Silence?
**SILENCE**
Good morrow, good cousin Shallow.
**SHALLOW**
And how doth my cousin, your bedfellow? and your
fairest daughter and mine, my god-daughter Ellen?
**SILENCE**
Alas, a black ousel, cousin Shallow!
**SHALLOW**
By yea and nay, sir, I dare say my cousin William is
become a good scholar: he is at Oxford still, is he not?
**SILENCE**
Indeed, sir, to my cost.
**SHALLOW**
A' must, then, to the inns o' court shortly. I was
once of Clement's Inn, where I think they will
talk of mad Shallow yet.
**SILENCE**
You were called 'lusty Shallow' then, cousin.
**SHALLOW**
By the mass, I was called any thing; and I would
have done any thing indeed too, and roundly too.
There was I, and little John Doit of Staffordshire,
and black George Barnes, and Francis Pickbone, and
Will Squele, a Cotswold man; you had not four such
swinge-bucklers in all the inns o' court again: and
I may say to you, we knew where the bona-robas were
and had the best of them all at commandment. Then
was Jack Falstaff, now Sir John, a boy, and page to
Thomas Mowbray, Duke of Norfolk.
**SILENCE**
This Sir John, cousin, that comes hither anon about soldiers?
**SHALLOW**
The same Sir John, the very same. I see him break
Skogan's head at the court-gate, when a' was a
crack not thus high: and the very same day did I
fight with one Sampson Stockfish, a fruiterer,
behind Gray's Inn. Jesu, Jesu, the mad days that I
have spent! and to see how many of my old
acquaintance are dead!
**SILENCE**
We shall all follow, cousin.
**SHADOW**
Certain, 'tis certain; very sure, very sure: death,
as the Psalmist saith, is certain to all; all shall
die. How a good yoke of bullocks at Stamford fair?
**SILENCE**
By my troth, I was not there.
**SHALLOW**
Death is certain. Is old Double of your town living
yet?
**SILENCE**

Dead, sir.
**SHALLOW**
Jesu, Jesu, dead! a' drew a good bow; and dead! a' shot a fine shoot: John a Gaunt loved him well, and betted much money on his head. Dead! a' would have clapped i' the clout at twelve score; and carried you a forehand shaft a fourteen and fourteen and a half, that it would have done a man's heart good to see. How a score of ewes now?
**SILENCE**
Thereafter as they be: a score of good ewes may be worth ten pounds.
**SHALLOW**
And is old Double dead?
**SILENCE**
Here come two of Sir John Falstaff's men, as I think.
*Enter BARDOLPH and one with him*
**BARDOLPH**
Good morrow, honest gentlemen: I beseech you, which is Justice Shallow?
**SHALLOW**
I am Robert Shallow, sir; a poor esquire of this county, and one of the king's justices of th e peace: What is your good pleasure with me?
**BARDOLPH**
My captain, sir, commends him to you; my captain, Sir John Falstaff, a tall gentleman, by heaven, and a most gallant leader.
**SHALLOW**
He greets me well, sir. I knew him a good backsword man. How doth the good knight? may I ask how my lady his wife doth?
**BARDOLPH**
Sir, pardon; a soldier is better accommodated than with a wife.
**SHALLOW**
It is well said, in faith, sir; and it is well said indeed too. Better accommodated! it is good; yea, indeed, is it: good phrases are surely, and ever were, very commendable. Accommodated! it comes of 'accommodo' very good; a good phrase.
**BARDOLPH**
Pardon me, sir; I have heard the word. Phrase call you it? by this good day, I know not the phrase; but I will maintain the word with my sword to be a soldier-like word, and a word of exceeding good command, by heaven. Accommodated; that is, when a man is, as they say, accommodated; or when a man is, being, whereby a' may be thought to be accommodated; which is an excellent thing.
**SHALLOW**
It is very just.
*Enter FALSTAFF*
Look, here comes good Sir John. Give me your good hand, give me your worship's good hand: by my troth, you like well and bear your years very well: welcome, good Sir John.
**FALSTAFF**
I am glad to see you well, good Master Robert Shallow: Master Surecard, as I think?
**SHALLOW**
No, Sir John; it is my cousin Silence, in commission with me.
**FALSTAFF**

Good Master Silence, it well befits you should be of the peace.

**SILENCE**

Your good-worship is welcome.

**FALSTAFF**

Fie! this is hot weather, gentlemen. Have you provided me here half a dozen sufficient men?

**SHALLOW**

Marry, have we, sir. Will you sit?

**FALSTAFF**

Let me see them, I beseech you.

**SHALLOW**

Where's the roll? where's the roll? where's the roll? Let me see, let me see, let me see. So, so: yea, marry, sir: Ralph Mouldy! Let them appear as I call; let them do so, let them do so. Let me see; where is Mouldy?

**MOULDY**

Here, an't please you.

**SHALLOW**

What think you, Sir John? a good-limbed fellow; young, strong, and of good friends.

**FALSTAFF**

Is thy name Mouldy?

**MOULDY**

Yea, an't please you.

**FALSTAFF**

'Tis the more time thou wert used.

**SHALLOW**

Ha, ha, ha! most excellent, i' faith! Things that are mouldy lack use: very singular good! in faith, well said, Sir John, very well said.

**FALSTAFF**

Prick him.

**MOULDY**

I was pricked well enough before, an you could have let me alone: my old dame will be undone now for one to do her husbandry and her drudgery: you need not to have pricked me; there are other men fitter to go out than I.

**FALSTAFF**

Go to: peace, Mouldy; you shall go. Mouldy, it is time you were spent.

**MOULDY**

Spent!

**SHALLOW**

Peace, fellow, peace; stand aside: know you where you are? For the other, Sir John: let me see: Simon Shadow!

**FALSTAFF**

Yea, marry, let me have him to sit under: he's like to be a cold soldier.

**SHALLOW**

Where's Shadow?

**SHADOW**

Here, sir.

**FALSTAFF**

Shadow, whose son art thou?

**SHADOW**

My mother's son, sir.

**FALSTAFF**

Thy mother's son! like enough, and thy father's shadow: so the son of the female is the shadow of

the male: it is often so, indeed; but much of the
father's substance!
**SHALLOW**
Do you like him, Sir John?
**FALSTAFF**
Shadow will serve for summer; prick him, for we have
a number of shadows to fill up the muster-book.
**SHALLOW**
Thomas Wart!
**FALSTAFF**
Where's he?
**WART**
Here, sir.
**FALSTAFF**
Is thy name Wart?
**WART**
Yea, sir.
**FALSTAFF**
Thou art a very ragged wart.
**SHALLOW**
Shall I prick him down, Sir John?
**FALSTAFF**
It were superfluous; for his apparel is built upon
his back and the whole frame stands upon pins:
prick him no more.
**SHALLOW**
Ha, ha, ha! you can do it, sir; you can do it: I
commend you well. Francis Feeble!
**FEEBLE**
Here, sir.
**FALSTAFF**
What trade art thou, Feeble?
**FEEBLE**
A woman's tailor, sir.
**SHALLOW**
Shall I prick him, sir?
**FALSTAFF**
You may: but if he had been a man's tailor, he'ld
ha' pricked you. Wilt thou make as many holes in
an enemy's battle as thou hast done in a woman's petticoat?
**FEEBLE**
I will do my good will, sir; you can have no more.
**FALSTAFF**
Well said, good woman's tailor! well said,
courageous Feeble! thou wilt be as valiant as the
wrathful dove or most magnanimous mouse. Prick the
woman's tailor: well, Master Shallow; deep, Master Shallow.
**FEEBLE**
I would Wart might have gone, sir.
**FALSTAFF**
I would thou wert a man's tailor, that thou mightst
mend him and make him fit to go. I cannot put him
to a private soldier that is the leader of so many
thousands: let that suffice, most forcible Feeble.
**FEEBLE**
It shall suffice, sir.
**FALSTAFF**
I am bound to thee, reverend Feeble. Who is next?
**SHALLOW**
Peter Bullcalf o' the green!
**FALSTAFF**
Yea, marry, let's see Bullcalf.
**BULLCALF**

Here, sir.
**FALSTAFF**
'Fore God, a likely fellow! Come, prick me Bullcalf
till he roar again.
**BULLCALF**
O Lord! good my lord captain,--
**FALSTAFF**
What, dost thou roar before thou art pricked?
**BULLCALF**
O Lord, sir! I am a diseased man.
**FALSTAFF**
What disease hast thou?
**BULLCALF**
A whoreson cold, sir, a cough, sir, which I caught
with ringing in the king's affairs upon his
coronation-day, sir.
**FALSTAFF**
Come, thou shalt go to the wars in a gown; we wilt
have away thy cold; and I will take such order that
my friends shall ring for thee. Is here all?
**SHALLOW**
Here is two more called than your number, you must
have but four here, sir: and so, I pray you, go in
with me to dinner.
**FALSTAFF**
Come, I will go drink with you, but I cannot tarry
dinner. I am glad to see you, by my troth, Master Shallow.
**SHALLOW**
O, Sir John, do you remember since we lay all night
in the windmill in Saint George's field?
**FALSTAFF**
No more of that, good Master Shallow, no more of that.
**SHALLOW**
Ha! 'twas a merry night. And is Jane Nightwork alive?
**FALSTAFF**
She lives, Master Shallow.
**SHALLOW**
She never could away with me.
**FALSTAFF**
Never, never; she would always say she could not
abide Master Shallow.
**SHALLOW**
By the mass, I could anger her to the heart. She
was then a bona-roba. Doth she hold her own well?
**FALSTAFF**
Old, old, Master Shallow.
**SHALLOW**
Nay, she must be old; she cannot choose but be old;
certain she's old; and had Robin Nightwork by old
Nightwork before I came to Clement's Inn.
**SILENCE**
That's fifty-five year ago.
**SHALLOW**
Ha, cousin Silence, that thou hadst seen that that
this knight and I have seen! Ha, Sir John, said I well?
**FALSTAFF**
We have heard the chimes at midnight, Master Shallow.
**SHALLOW**
That we have, that we have, that we have; in faith,
Sir John, we have: our watch-word was 'Hem boys!'
Come, let's to dinner; come, let's to dinner:
Jesus, the days that we have seen! Come, come.
*Exeunt FALSTAFF and Justices*

**BULLCALF**
Good Master Corporate Bardolph, stand my friend; and here's four Harry ten shillings in French crowns for you. In very truth, sir, I had as lief be hanged, sir, as go: and yet, for mine own part, sir, I do not care; but rather, because I am unwilling, and, for mine own part, have a desire to stay with my friends; else, sir, I did not care, for mine own part, so much.
**BARDOLPH**
Go to; stand aside.
**MOULDY**
And, good master corporal captain, for my old dame's sake, stand my friend: she has nobody to do any thing about her when I am gone; and she is old, and cannot help herself: You shall have forty, sir.
**BARDOLPH**
Go to; stand aside.
**FEEBLE**
By my troth, I care not; a man can die but once: we owe God a death: I'll ne'er bear a base mind: an't be my destiny, so; an't be not, so: no man is too good to serve's prince; and let it go which way it will, he that dies this year is quit for the next.
**BARDOLPH**
Well said; thou'rt a good fellow.
**FEEBLE**
Faith, I'll bear no base mind.
*Re-enter FALSTAFF and the Justices*
**FALSTAFF**
Come, sir, which men shall I have?
**SHALLOW**
Four of which you please.
**BARDOLPH**
Sir, a word with you: I have three pound to free Mouldy and Bullcalf.
**FALSTAFF**
Go to; well.
**SHALLOW**
Come, Sir John, which four will you have?
**FALSTAFF**
Do you choose for me.
**SHALLOW**
Marry, then, Mouldy, Bullcalf, Feeble and Shadow.
**FALSTAFF**
Mouldy and Bullcalf: for you, Mouldy, stay at home till you are past service: and for your part, Bullcalf, grow till you come unto it: I will none of you.
**SHALLOW**
Sir John, Sir John, do not yourself wrong: they are your likeliest men, and I would have you served with the best.
**FALSTAFF**
Will you tell me, Master Shallow, how to choose a man? Care I for the limb, the thewes, the stature, bulk, and big assemblance of a man! Give me the spirit, Master Shallow. Here's Wart; you see what a ragged appearance it is; a' shall charge you and discharge you with the motion of a pewterer's hammer, come off and on swifter than he that gibbets on the brewer's bucket. And this same half-faced fellow, Shadow; give me this man: he presents no mark to the enemy; the foeman may with as great aim level at the edge of a penknife. And for a retreat;

how swiftly will this Feeble the woman's tailor run off! O, give me the spare men, and spare me the great ones. Put me a caliver into Wart's hand, Bardolph.
**BARDOLPH**
Hold, Wart, traverse; thus, thus, thus.
**FALSTAFF**
Come, manage me your caliver. So: very well: go to: very good, exceeding good. O, give me always a little, lean, old, chapt, bald shot. Well said, i' faith, Wart; thou'rt a good scab: hold, there's a tester for thee.
**SHALLOW**
He is not his craft's master; he doth not do it right. I remember at Mile-end Green, when I lay at Clement's Inn--I was then Sir Dagonet in Arthur's show,--there was a little quiver fellow, and a' would manage you his piece thus; and a' would about and about, and come you in and come you in: 'rah, tah, tah,' would a' say; 'bounce' would a' say; and away again would a' go, and again would a' come: I shall ne'er see such a fellow.
**FALSTAFF**
These fellows will do well, Master Shallow. God keep you, Master Silence: I will not use many words with you. Fare you well, gentlemen both: I thank you: I must a dozen mile to-night. Bardolph, give the soldiers coats.
**SHALLOW**
Sir John, the Lord bless you! God prosper your affairs! God send us peace! At your return visit our house; let our old acquaintance be renewed; peradventure I will with ye to the court.
**FALSTAFF**
'Fore God, I would you would, Master Shallow.
**SHALLOW**
Go to; I have spoke at a word. God keep you.
**FALSTAFF**
Fare you well, gentle gentlemen.
*Exeunt Justices*
On, Bardolph; lead the men away.
*Exeunt BARDOLPH, Recruits, &c*
As I return, I will fetch off these justices: I do see the bottom of Justice Shallow. Lord, Lord, how subject we old men are to this vice of lying! This same starved justice hath done nothing but prate to me of the wildness of his youth, and the feats he hath done about Turnbull Street: and every third word a lie, duer paid to the hearer than the Turk's tribute. I do remember him at Clement's Inn like a man made after supper of a cheese-paring: when a' was naked, he was, for all the world, like a forked radish, with a head fantastically carved upon it with a knife: a' was so forlorn, that his dimensions to any thick sight were invincible: a' was the very genius of famine; yet lecherous as a monkey, and the whores called him mandrake: a' came ever in the rearward of the fashion, and sung those tunes to the overscutched huswives that he heard the carmen whistle, and swear they were his fancies or his good-nights. And now is this Vice's dagger become a squire, and talks as familiarly of John a Gaunt as if he had been sworn brother to him; and I'll be sworn a' ne'er saw him but once in the

Tilt-yard; and then he burst his head for crowding among the marshal's men. I saw it, and told John a Gaunt he beat his own name; for you might have thrust him and all his apparel into an eel-skin; the case of a treble hautboy was a mansion for him, a court: and now has he land and beefs. Well, I'll be acquainted with him, if I return; and it shall go hard but I will make him a philosopher's two stones to me: if the young dace be a bait for the old pike, I see no reason in the law of nature but I may snap at him. Let time shape, and there an end. *Exit*

## ACT IV

**SCENE I. Yorkshire. Gaultree Forest.**

*Enter the ARCHBISHOP OF YORK, MOWBRAY, LORD HASTINGS, and others*

**ARCHBISHOP OF YORK**

What is this forest call'd?

**HASTINGS**

'Tis Gaultree Forest, an't shall please your grace.

**ARCHBISHOP OF YORK**

Here stand, my lords; and send discoverers forth
To know the numbers of our enemies.

**HASTINGS**

We have sent forth already.

**ARCHBISHOP OF YORK**

'Tis well done.
My friends and brethren in these great affairs,
I must acquaint you that I have received
New-dated letters from Northumberland;
Their cold intent, tenor and substance, thus:
Here doth he wish his person, with such powers
As might hold sortance with his quality,
The which he could not levy; whereupon
He is retired, to ripe his growing fortunes,
To Scotland: and concludes in hearty prayers
That your attempts may overlive the hazard
And fearful melting of their opposite.

**MOWBRAY**

Thus do the hopes we have in him touch ground
And dash themselves to pieces.

*Enter a Messenger*

**HASTINGS**

Now, what news?

**Messenger**

West of this forest, scarcely off a mile,
In goodly form comes on the enemy;
And, by the ground they hide, I judge their number
Upon or near the rate of thirty thousand.

**MOWBRAY**

The just proportion that we gave them out
Let us sway on and face them in the field.

**ARCHBISHOP OF YORK**

What well-appointed leader fronts us here?

*Enter WESTMORELAND*

**MOWBRAY**

I think it is my Lord of Westmoreland.

**WESTMORELAND**

Health and fair greeting from our general,
The prince, Lord John and Duke of Lancaster.

**ARCHBISHOP OF YORK**

Say on, my Lord of Westmoreland, in peace:
What doth concern your coming?

**WESTMORELAND**

Then, my lord,
Unto your grace do I in chief address
The substance of my speech. If that rebellion
Came like itself, in base and abject routs,
Led on by bloody youth, guarded with rags,
And countenanced by boys and beggary,
I say, if damn'd commotion so appear'd,
In his true, native and most proper shape,
You, reverend father, and these noble lords
Had not been here, to dress the ugly form
Of base and bloody insurrection
With your fair honours. You, lord archbishop,

Whose see is by a civil peace maintained,
Whose beard the silver hand of peace hath touch'd,
Whose learning and good letters peace hath tutor'd,
Whose white investments figure innocence,
The dove and very blessed spirit of peace,
Wherefore do you so ill translate ourself
Out of the speech of peace that bears such grace,
Into the harsh and boisterous tongue of war;
Turning your books to graves, your ink to blood,
Your pens to lances and your tongue divine
To a trumpet and a point of war?
**ARCHBISHOP OF YORK**
Wherefore do I this? so the question stands.
Briefly to this end: we are all diseased,
And with our surfeiting and wanton hours
Have brought ourselves into a burning fever,
And we must bleed for it; of which disease
Our late king, Richard, being infected, died.
But, my most noble Lord of Westmoreland,
I take not on me here as a physician,
Nor do I as an enemy to peace
Troop in the throngs of military men;
But rather show awhile like fearful war,
To diet rank minds sick of happiness
And purge the obstructions which begin to stop
Our very veins of life. Hear me more plainly.
I have in equal balance justly weigh'd
What wrongs our arms may do, what wrongs we suffer,
And find our griefs heavier than our offences.
We see which way the stream of time doth run,
And are enforced from our most quiet there
By the rough torrent of occasion;
And have the summary of all our griefs,
When time shall serve, to show in articles;
Which long ere this we offer'd to the king,
And might by no suit gain our audience:
When we are wrong'd and would unfold our griefs,
We are denied access unto his person
Even by those men that most have done us wrong.
The dangers of the days but newly gone,
Whose memory is written on the earth
With yet appearing blood, and the examples
Of every minute's instance, present now,
Hath put us in these ill-beseeming arms,
Not to break peace or any branch of it,
But to establish here a peace indeed,
Concurring both in name and quality.
**WESTMORELAND**
When ever yet was your appeal denied?
Wherein have you been galled by the king?
What peer hath been suborn'd to grate on you,
That you should seal this lawless bloody book
Of forged rebellion with a seal divine
And consecrate commotion's bitter edge?
**ARCHBISHOP OF YORK**
My brother general, the commonwealth,
To brother born an household cruelty,
I make my quarrel in particular.
**WESTMORELAND**
There is no need of any such redress;
Or if there were, it not belongs to you.
**MOWBRAY**

Why not to him in part, and to us all
That feel the bruises of the days before,
And suffer the condition of these times
To lay a heavy and unequal hand
Upon our honours?
**WESTMORELAND**
O, my good Lord Mowbray,
Construe the times to their necessities,
And you shall say indeed, it is the time,
And not the king, that doth you injuries.
Yet for your part, it not appears to me
Either from the king or in the present time
That you should have an inch of any ground
To build a grief on: were you not restored
To all the Duke of Norfolk's signories,
Your noble and right well remember'd father's?
**MOWBRAY**
What thing, in honour, had my father lost,
That need to be revived and breathed in me?
The king that loved him, as the state stood then,
Was force perforce compell'd to banish him:
And then that Harry Bolingbroke and he,
Being mounted and both roused in their seats,
Their neighing coursers daring of the spur,
Their armed staves in charge, their beavers down,
Their eyes of fire sparking through sights of steel
And the loud trumpet blowing them together,
Then, then, when there was nothing could have stay'd
My father from the breast of Bolingbroke,
O when the king did throw his warder down,
His own life hung upon the staff he threw;
Then threw he down himself and all their lives
That by indictment and by dint of sword
Have since miscarried under Bolingbroke.
**WESTMORELAND**
You speak, Lord Mowbray, now you know not what.
The Earl of Hereford was reputed then
In England the most valiant gentlemen:
Who knows on whom fortune would then have smiled?
But if your father had been victor there,
He ne'er had borne it out of Coventry:
For all the country in a general voice
Cried hate upon him; and all their prayers and love
Were set on Hereford, whom they doted on
And bless'd and graced indeed, more than the king.
But this is mere digression from my purpose.
Here come I from our princely general
To know your griefs; to tell you from his grace
That he will give you audience; and wherein
It shall appear that your demands are just,
You shall enjoy them, every thing set off
That might so much as think you enemies.
**MOWBRAY**
But he hath forced us to compel this offer;
And it proceeds from policy, not love.
**WESTMORELAND**
Mowbray, you overween to take it so;
This offer comes from mercy, not from fear:
For, lo! within a ken our army lies,
Upon mine honour, all too confident
To give admittance to a thought of fear.
Our battle is more full of names than yours,
Our men more perfect in the use of arms,

Our armour all as strong, our cause the best;
Then reason will our heart should be as good
Say you not then our offer is compell'd.
**MOWBRAY**
Well, by my will we shall admit no parley.
**WESTMORELAND**
That argues but the shame of your offence:
A rotten case abides no handling.
**HASTINGS**
Hath the Prince John a full commission,
In very ample virtue of his father,
To hear and absolutely to determine
Of what conditions we shall stand upon?
**WESTMORELAND**
That is intended in the general's name:
I muse you make so slight a question.
**ARCHBISHOP OF YORK**
Then take, my Lord of Westmoreland, this schedule,
For this contains our general grievances:
Each several article herein redress'd,
All members of our cause, both here and hence,
That are insinew'd to this action,
Acquitted by a true substantial form
And present execution of our wills
To us and to our purposes confined,
We come within our awful banks again
And knit our powers to the arm of peace.
**WESTMORELAND**
This will I show the general. Please you, lords,
In sight of both our battles we may meet;
And either end in peace, which God so frame!
Or to the place of difference call the swords
Which must decide it.
**ARCHBISHOP OF YORK**
My lord, we will do so.
*Exit WESTMORELAND*
**MOWBRAY**
There is a thing within my bosom tells me
That no conditions of our peace can stand.
**HASTINGS**
Fear you not that: if we can make our peace
Upon such large terms and so absolute
As our conditions shall consist upon,
Our peace shall stand as firm as rocky mountains.
**MOWBRAY**
Yea, but our valuation shall be such
That every slight and false-derived cause,
Yea, every idle, nice and wanton reason
Shall to the king taste of this action;
That, were our royal faiths martyrs in love,
We shall be winnow'd with so rough a wind
That even our corn shall seem as light as chaff
And good from bad find no partition.
**ARCHBISHOP OF YORK**
No, no, my lord. Note this; the king is weary
Of dainty and such picking grievances:
For he hath found to end one doubt by death
Revives two greater in the heirs of life,
And therefore will he wipe his tables clean
And keep no tell-tale to his memory
That may repeat and history his loss
To new remembrance; for full well he knows
He cannot so precisely weed this land

As his misdoubts present occasion:
His foes are so enrooted with his friends
That, plucking to unfix an enemy,
He doth unfasten so and shake a friend:
So that this land, like an offensive wife
That hath enraged him on to offer strokes,
As he is striking, holds his infant up
And hangs resolved correction in the arm
That was uprear'd to execution.

**HASTINGS**

Besides, the king hath wasted all his rods
On late offenders, that he now doth lack
The very instruments of chastisement:
So that his power, like to a fangless lion,
May offer, but not hold.

**ARCHBISHOP OF YORK**

'Tis very true:
And therefore be assured, my good lord marshal,
If we do now make our atonement well,
Our peace will, like a broken limb united,
Grow stronger for the breaking.

**MOWBRAY**

Be it so.
Here is return'd my Lord of Westmoreland.
*Re-enter WESTMORELAND*

**WESTMORELAND**

The prince is here at hand: pleaseth your lordship
To meet his grace just distance 'tween our armies.

**MOWBRAY**

Your grace of York, in God's name then, set forward.

**ARCHBISHOP OF YORK**

Before, and greet his grace: my lord, we come.
*Exeunt*

**SCENE II. Another part of the forest.**

*Enter, from one side, MOWBRAY, attended; afterwards the ARCHBISHOP OF YORK, HASTINGS, and others: from the other side, Prince John of LANCASTER, and WESTMORELAND; Officers, and others with them*

**LANCASTER**

You are well encounter'd here, my cousin Mowbray:
Good day to you, gentle lord archbishop;
And so to you, Lord Hastings, and to all.
My Lord of York, it better show'd with you
When that your flock, assembled by the bell,
Encircled you to hear with reverence
Your exposition on the holy text
Than now to see you here an iron man,
Cheering a rout of rebels with your drum,
Turning the word to sword and life to death.
That man that sits within a monarch's heart,
And ripens in the sunshine of his favour,
Would he abuse the countenance of the king,
Alack, what mischiefs might he set abrooch
In shadow of such greatness! With you, lord bishop,
It is even so. Who hath not heard it spoken
How deep you were within the books of God?
To us the speaker in his parliament;
To us the imagined voice of God himself;
The very opener and intelligencer
Between the grace, the sanctities of heaven
And our dull workings. O, who shall believe
But you misuse the reverence of your place,
Employ the countenance and grace of heaven,
As a false favourite doth his prince's name,

In deeds dishonourable? You have ta'en up,
Under the counterfeited zeal of God,
The subjects of his substitute, my father,
And both against the peace of heaven and him
Have here up-swarm'd them.

**ARCHBISHOP OF YORK**

Good my Lord of Lancaster,
I am not here against your father's peace;
But, as I told my lord of Westmoreland,
The time misorder'd doth, in common sense,
Crowd us and crush us to this monstrous form,
To hold our safety up. I sent your grace
The parcels and particulars of our grief,
The which hath been with scorn shoved from the court,
Whereon this Hydra son of war is born;
Whose dangerous eyes may well be charm'd asleep
With grant of our most just and right desires,
And true obedience, of this madness cured,
Stoop tamely to the foot of majesty.

**MOWBRAY**

If not, we ready are to try our fortunes
To the last man.

**HASTINGS**

And though we here fall down,
We have supplies to second our attempt:
If they miscarry, theirs shall second them;
And so success of mischief shall be born
And heir from heir shall hold this quarrel up
Whiles England shall have generation.

**LANCASTER**

You are too shallow, Hastings, much too shallow,
To sound the bottom of the after-times.

**WESTMORELAND**

Pleaseth your grace to answer them directly
How far forth you do like their articles.

**LANCASTER**

I like them all, and do allow them well,
And swear here, by the honour of my blood,
My father's purposes have been mistook,
And some about him have too lavishly
Wrested his meaning and authority.
My lord, these griefs shall be with speed redress'd;
Upon my soul, they shall. If this may please you,
Discharge your powers unto their several counties,
As we will ours: and here between the armies
Let's drink together friendly and embrace,
That all their eyes may bear those tokens home
Of our restored love and amity.

**ARCHBISHOP OF YORK**

I take your princely word for these redresses.

**LANCASTER**

I give it you, and will maintain my word:
And thereupon I drink unto your grace.

**HASTINGS**

Go, captain, and deliver to the army
This news of peace: let them have pay, and part:
I know it will well please them. Hie thee, captain.
*Exit Officer*

**ARCHBISHOP OF YORK**

To you, my noble Lord of Westmoreland.

**WESTMORELAND**

I pledge your grace; and, if you knew what pains
I have bestow'd to breed this present peace,

You would drink freely: but my love to ye
Shall show itself more openly hereafter.
**ARCHBISHOP OF YORK**
I do not doubt you.
**WESTMORELAND**
I am glad of it.
Health to my lord and gentle cousin, Mowbray.
**MOWBRAY**
You wish me health in very happy season;
For I am, on the sudden, something ill.
**ARCHBISHOP OF YORK**
Against ill chances men are ever merry;
But heaviness foreruns the good event.
**WESTMORELAND**
Therefore be merry, coz; since sudden sorrow
Serves to say thus, 'some good thing comes
to-morrow.'
**ARCHBISHOP OF YORK**
Believe me, I am passing light in spirit.
**MOWBRAY**
So much the worse, if your own rule be true.
*Shouts within*
**LANCASTER**
The word of peace is render'd: hark, how they shout!
**MOWBRAY**
This had been cheerful after victory.
**ARCHBISHOP OF YORK**
A peace is of the nature of a conquest;
For then both parties nobly are subdued,
And neither party loser.
**LANCASTER**
Go, my lord,
And let our army be discharged too.
*Exit WESTMORELAND*
And, good my lord, so please you, let our trains
March, by us, that we may peruse the men
We should have coped withal.
**ARCHBISHOP OF YORK**
Go, good Lord Hastings,
And, ere they be dismissed, let them march by.
*Exit HASTINGS*
**LANCASTER**
I trust, lords, we shall lie to-night together.
*Re-enter WESTMORELAND*
Now, cousin, wherefore stands our army still?
**WESTMORELAND**
The leaders, having charge from you to stand,
Will not go off until they hear you speak.
**LANCASTER**
They know their duties.
*Re-enter HASTINGS*
**HASTINGS**
My lord, our army is dispersed already;
Like youthful steers unyoked, they take their courses
East, west, north, south; or, like a school broke up,
Each hurries toward his home and sporting-place.
**WESTMORELAND**
Good tidings, my Lord Hastings; for the which
I do arrest thee, traitor, of high treason:
And you, lord archbishop, and you, Lord Mowbray,
Of capitol treason I attach you both.
**MOWBRAY**
Is this proceeding just and honourable?

**WESTMORELAND**
Is your assembly so?
**ARCHBISHOP OF YORK**
Will you thus break your faith?
**LANCASTER**
I pawn'd thee none:
I promised you redress of these same grievances
Whereof you did complain; which, by mine honour,
I will perform with a most Christian care.
But for you, rebels, look to taste the due
Meet for rebellion and such acts as yours.
Most shallowly did you these arms commence,
Fondly brought here and foolishly sent hence.
Strike up our drums, pursue the scatter'd stray:
God, and not we, hath safely fought to-day.
Some guard these traitors to the block of death,
Treason's true bed and yielder up of breath.
*Exeunt*
**SCENE III. Another part of the forest.**
*Alarum. Excursions. Enter FALSTAFF and COLEVILE, meeting*
**FALSTAFF**
What's your name, sir? of what condition are you,
and of what place, I pray?
**COLEVILE**
I am a knight, sir, and my name is Colevile of the dale.
**FALSTAFF**
Well, then, Colevile is your name, a knight is your
degree, and your place the dale: Colevile shall be
still your name, a traitor your degree, and the
dungeon your place, a place deep enough; so shall
you be still Colevile of the dale.
**COLEVILE**
Are not you Sir John Falstaff?
**FALSTAFF**
As good a man as he, sir, whoe'er I am. Do ye
yield, sir? or shall I sweat for you? if I do
sweat, they are the drops of thy lovers, and they
weep for thy death: therefore rouse up fear and
trembling, and do observance to my mercy.
**COLEVILE**
I think you are Sir John Falstaff, and in that
thought yield me.
**FALSTAFF**
I have a whole school of tongues in this belly of
mine, and not a tongue of them all speaks any other
word but my name. An I had but a belly of any
indifference, I were simply the most active fellow
in Europe: my womb, my womb, my womb, undoes me.
Here comes our general.
*Enter PRINCE JOHN OF LANCASTER, WESTMORELAND, BLUNT, and others*
**LANCASTER**
The heat is past; follow no further now:
Call in the powers, good cousin Westmoreland.
*Exit WESTMORELAND*
Now, Falstaff, where have you been all this while?
When every thing is ended, then you come:
These tardy tricks of yours will, on my life,
One time or other break some gallows' back.
**FALSTAFF**
I would be sorry, my lord, but it should be thus: I
never knew yet but rebuke and cheque was the reward
of valour. Do you think me a swallow, an arrow, or a
bullet? have I, in my poor and old motion, the

expedition of thought? I have speeded hither with
the very extremest inch of possibility; I have
foundered nine score and odd posts: and here,
travel-tainted as I am, have in my pure and
immaculate valour, taken Sir John Colevile of the
dale, a most furious knight and valorous enemy.
But what of that? he saw me, and yielded; that I
may justly say, with the hook-nosed fellow of Rome,
'I came, saw, and overcame.'
**LANCASTER**
It was more of his courtesy than your deserving.
**FALSTAFF**
I know not: here he is, and here I yield him: and
I beseech your grace, let it be booked with the
rest of this day's deeds; or, by the Lord, I will
have it in a particular ballad else, with mine own
picture on the top on't, Colevile kissing my foot:
to the which course if I be enforced, if you do not
all show like gilt twopences to me, and I in the
clear sky of fame o'ershine you as much as the full
moon doth the cinders of the element, which show
like pins' heads to her, believe not the word of
the noble: therefore let me have right, and let
desert mount.
**LANCASTER**
Thine's too heavy to mount.
**FALSTAFF**
Let it shine, then.
**LANCASTER**
Thine's too thick to shine.
**FALSTAFF**
Let it do something, my good lord, that may do me
good, and call it what you will.
**LANCASTER**
Is thy name Colevile?
**COLEVILE**
It is, my lord.
**LANCASTER**
A famous rebel art thou, Colevile.
**FALSTAFF**
And a famous true subject took him.
**COLEVILE**
I am, my lord, but as my betters are
That led me hither: had they been ruled by me,
You should have won them dearer than you have.
**FALSTAFF**
I know not how they sold themselves: but thou, like
a kind fellow, gavest thyself away gratis; and I
thank thee for thee.
*Re-enter WESTMORELAND*
**LANCASTER**
Now, have you left pursuit?
**WESTMORELAND**
Retreat is made and execution stay'd.
**LANCASTER**
Send Colevile with his confederates
To York, to present execution:
Blunt, lead him hence; and see you guard him sure.
*Exeunt BLUNT and others with COLEVILE*
And now dispatch we toward the court, my lords:
I hear the king my father is sore sick:
Our news shall go before us to his majesty,

Which, cousin, you shall bear to comfort him,
And we with sober speed will follow you.

**FALSTAFF**

My lord, I beseech you, give me leave to go
Through Gloucestershire: and, when you come to court,
Stand my good lord, pray, in your good report.

**LANCASTER**

Fare you well, Falstaff: I, in my condition,
Shall better speak of you than you deserve.
*Exeunt all but Falstaff*

**FALSTAFF**

I would you had but the wit: 'twere better than
your dukedom. Good faith, this same young sober-
blooded boy doth not love me; nor a man cannot make
him laugh; but that's no marvel, he drinks no wine.
There's never none of these demure boys come to any
proof; for thin drink doth so over-cool their blood,
and making many fish-meals, that they fall into a
kind of male green-sickness; and then when they
marry, they get wenches: they are generally fools
and cowards; which some of us should be too, but for
inflammation. A good sherris sack hath a two-fold
operation in it. It ascends me into the brain;
dries me there all the foolish and dull and curdy
vapours which environ it; makes it apprehensive,
quick, forgetive, full of nimble fiery and
delectable shapes, which, delivered o'er to the
voice, the tongue, which is the birth, becomes
excellent wit. The second property of your
excellent sherris is, the warming of the blood;
which, before cold and settled, left the liver
white and pale, which is the badge of pusillanimity
and cowardice; but the sherris warms it and makes
it course from the inwards to the parts extreme:
it illumineth the face, which as a beacon gives
warning to all the rest of this little kingdom,
man, to arm; and then the vital commoners and
inland petty spirits muster me all to their captain,
the heart, who, great and puffed up with this
retinue, doth any deed of courage; and this valour
comes of sherris. So that skill in the weapon is
nothing without sack, for that sets it a-work; and
learning a mere hoard of gold kept by a devil, till
sack commences it and sets it in act and use.
Hereof comes it that Prince Harry is valiant; for
the cold blood he did naturally inherit of his
father, he hath, like lean, sterile and bare land,
manured, husbanded and tilled with excellent
endeavour of drinking good and good store of fertile
sherris, that he is become very hot and valiant. If
I had a thousand sons, the first humane principle I
would teach them should be, to forswear thin
potations and to addict themselves to sack.
*Enter BARDOLPH*
How now Bardolph?

**BARDOLPH**

The army is discharged all and gone.

**FALSTAFF**

Let them go. I'll through Gloucestershire; and
there will I visit Master Robert Shallow, esquire:
I have him already tempering between my finger and
my thumb, and shortly will I seal with him. Come away.
*Exeunt*

**SCENE IV. Westminster. The Jerusalem Chamber.**

*Enter KING HENRY IV, the Princes Thomas of CLARENCE and Humphrey of GLOUCESTER, WARWICK, and others*

**KING HENRY IV**

Now, lords, if God doth give successful end
To this debate that bleedeth at our doors,
We will our youth lead on to higher fields
And draw no swords but what are sanctified.
Our navy is address'd, our power collected,
Our substitutes in absence well invested,
And every thing lies level to our wish:
Only, we want a little personal strength;
And pause us, till these rebels, now afoot,
Come underneath the yoke of government.

**WARWICK**

Both which we doubt not but your majesty
Shall soon enjoy.

**KING HENRY IV**

Humphrey, my son of Gloucester,
Where is the prince your brother?

**GLOUCESTER**

I think he's gone to hunt, my lord, at Windsor.

**KING HENRY IV**

And how accompanied?

**GLOUCESTER**

I do not know, my lord.

**KING HENRY IV**

Is not his brother, Thomas of Clarence, with him?

**GLOUCESTER**

No, my good lord; he is in presence here.

**CLARENCE**

What would my lord and father?

**KING HENRY IV**

Nothing but well to thee, Thomas of Clarence.
How chance thou art not with the prince thy brother?
He loves thee, and thou dost neglect him, Thomas;
Thou hast a better place in his affection
Than all thy brothers: cherish it, my boy,
And noble offices thou mayst effect
Of mediation, after I am dead,
Between his greatness and thy other brethren:
Therefore omit him not; blunt not his love,
Nor lose the good advantage of his grace
By seeming cold or careless of his will;
For he is gracious, if he be observed:
He hath a tear for pity and a hand
Open as day for melting charity:
Yet notwithstanding, being incensed, he's flint,
As humorous as winter and as sudden
As flaws congealed in the spring of day.
His temper, therefore, must be well observed:
Chide him for faults, and do it reverently,
When thou perceive his blood inclined to mirth;
But, being moody, give him line and scope,
Till that his passions, like a whale on ground,
Confound themselves with working. Learn this, Thomas,
And thou shalt prove a shelter to thy friends,
A hoop of gold to bind thy brothers in,
That the united vessel of their blood,
Mingled with venom of suggestion--
As, force perforce, the age will pour it in--
Shall never leak, though it do work as strong
As aconitum or rash gunpowder.

**CLARENCE**
I shall observe him with all care and love.
**KING HENRY IV**
Why art thou not at Windsor with him, Thomas?
**CLARENCE**
He is not there to-day; he dines in London.
**KING HENRY IV**
And how accompanied? canst thou tell that?
**CLARENCE**
With Poins, and other his continual followers.
**KING HENRY IV**
Most subject is the fattest soil to weeds;
And he, the noble image of my youth,
Is overspread with them: therefore my grief
Stretches itself beyond the hour of death:
The blood weeps from my heart when I do shape
In forms imaginary the unguided days
And rotten times that you shall look upon
When I am sleeping with my ancestors.
For when his headstrong riot hath no curb,
When rage and hot blood are his counsellors,
When means and lavish manners meet together,
O, with what wings shall his affections fly
Towards fronting peril and opposed decay!
**WARWICK**
My gracious lord, you look beyond him quite:
The prince but studies his companions
Like a strange tongue, wherein, to gain the language,
'Tis needful that the most immodest word
Be look'd upon and learn'd; which once attain'd,
Your highness knows, comes to no further use
But to be known and hated. So, like gross terms,
The prince will in the perfectness of time
Cast off his followers; and their memory
Shall as a pattern or a measure live,
By which his grace must mete the lives of others,
Turning past evils to advantages.
**KING HENRY IV**
'Tis seldom when the bee doth leave her comb
In the dead carrion.
*Enter WESTMORELAND*
Who's here? Westmoreland?
**WESTMORELAND**
Health to my sovereign, and new happiness
Added to that that I am to deliver!
Prince John your son doth kiss your grace's hand:
Mowbray, the Bishop Scroop, Hastings and all
Are brought to the correction of your law;
There is not now a rebel's sword unsheath'd
But peace puts forth her olive every where.
The manner how this action hath been borne
Here at more leisure may your highness read,
With every course in his particular.
**KING HENRY IV**
O Westmoreland, thou art a summer bird,
Which ever in the haunch of winter sings
The lifting up of day.
*Enter HARCOURT*
Look, here's more news.
**HARCOURT**
From enemies heaven keep your majesty;
And, when they stand against you, may they fall
As those that I am come to tell you of!

The Earl Northumberland and the Lord Bardolph,
With a great power of English and of Scots
Are by the sheriff of Yorkshire overthrown:
The manner and true order of the fight
This packet, please it you, contains at large.
**KING HENRY IV**
And wherefore should these good news make me sick?
Will fortune never come with both hands full,
But write her fair words still in foulest letters?
She either gives a stomach and no food;
Such are the poor, in health; or else a feast
And takes away the stomach; such are the rich,
That have abundance and enjoy it not.
I should rejoice now at this happy news;
And now my sight fails, and my brain is giddy:
O me! come near me; now I am much ill.
**GLOUCESTER**
Comfort, your majesty!
**CLARENCE**
O my royal father!
**WESTMORELAND**
My sovereign lord, cheer up yourself, look up.
**WARWICK**
Be patient, princes; you do know, these fits
Are with his highness very ordinary.
Stand from him. Give him air; he'll straight be well.
**CLARENCE**
No, no, he cannot long hold out these pangs:
The incessant care and labour of his mind
Hath wrought the mure that should confine it in
So thin that life looks through and will break out.
**GLOUCESTER**
The people fear me; for they do observe
Unfather'd heirs and loathly births of nature:
The seasons change their manners, as the year
Had found some months asleep and leap'd them over.
**CLARENCE**
The river hath thrice flow'd, no ebb between;
And the old folk, time's doting chronicles,
Say it did so a little time before
That our great-grandsire, Edward, sick'd and died.
**WARWICK**
Speak lower, princes, for the king recovers.
**GLOUCESTER**
This apoplexy will certain be his end.
**KING HENRY IV**
I pray you, take me up, and bear me hence
Into some other chamber: softly, pray.
**SCENE V. Another chamber.**
*KING HENRY IV lying on a bed: CLARENCE, GLOUCESTER, WARWICK, and others in attendance*
**KING HENRY IV**
Let there be no noise made, my gentle friends;
Unless some dull and favourable hand
Will whisper music to my weary spirit.
**WARWICK**
Call for the music in the other room.
**KING HENRY IV**
Set me the crown upon my pillow here.
**CLARENCE**
His eye is hollow, and he changes much.
**WARWICK**
Less noise, less noise!
*Enter PRINCE HENRY*

**PRINCE HENRY**
Who saw the Duke of Clarence?
**CLARENCE**
I am here, brother, full of heaviness.
**PRINCE HENRY**
How now! rain within doors, and none abroad!
How doth the king?
**GLOUCESTER**
Exceeding ill.
**PRINCE HENRY**
Heard he the good news yet?
Tell it him.
**GLOUCESTER**
He alter'd much upon the hearing it.
**PRINCE HENRY**
If he be sick with joy, he'll recover without physic.
**WARWICK**
Not so much noise, my lords: sweet prince,
speak low;
The king your father is disposed to sleep.
**CLARENCE**
Let us withdraw into the other room.
**WARWICK**
Will't please your grace to go along with us?
**PRINCE HENRY**
No; I will sit and watch here by the king.
*Exeunt all but PRINCE HENRY*
Why doth the crown lie there upon his pillow,
Being so troublesome a bedfellow?
O polish'd perturbation! golden care!
That keep'st the ports of slumber open wide
To many a watchful night! sleep with it now!
Yet not so sound and half so deeply sweet
As he whose brow with homely biggen bound
Snores out the watch of night. O majesty!
When thou dost pinch thy bearer, thou dost sit
Like a rich armour worn in heat of day,
That scalds with safety. By his gates of breath
There lies a downy feather which stirs not:
Did he suspire, that light and weightless down
Perforce must move. My gracious lord! my father!
This sleep is sound indeed, this is a sleep
That from this golden rigol hath divorced
So many English kings. Thy due from me
Is tears and heavy sorrows of the blood,
Which nature, love, and filial tenderness,
Shall, O dear father, pay thee plenteously:
My due from thee is this imperial crown,
Which, as immediate as thy place and blood,
Derives itself to me. Lo, here it sits,
Which God shall guard: and put the world's whole strength
Into one giant arm, it shall not force
This lineal honour from me: this from thee
Will I to mine leave, as 'tis left to me.
*Exit*
**KING HENRY IV**
Warwick! Gloucester! Clarence!
*Re-enter WARWICK, GLOUCESTER, CLARENCE, and the rest*
**CLARENCE**
Doth the king call?
**WARWICK**
What would your majesty? How fares your grace?
**KING HENRY IV**

Why did you leave me here alone, my lords?
**CLARENCE**
We left the prince my brother here, my liege,
Who undertook to sit and watch by you.
**KING HENRY IV**
The Prince of Wales! Where is he? let me see him:
He is not here.
**WARWICK**
This door is open; he is gone this way.
**GLOUCESTER**
He came not through the chamber where we stay'd.
**KING HENRY IV**
Where is the crown? who took it from my pillow?
**WARWICK**
When we withdrew, my liege, we left it here.
**KING HENRY IV**
The prince hath ta'en it hence: go, seek him out.
Is he so hasty that he doth suppose
My sleep my death?
Find him, my Lord of Warwick; chide him hither.
*Exit WARWICK*
This part of his conjoins with my disease,
And helps to end me. See, sons, what things you are!
How quickly nature falls into revolt
When gold becomes her object!
For this the foolish over-careful fathers
Have broke their sleep with thoughts, their brains with care,
Their bones with industry;
For this they have engrossed and piled up
The canker'd heaps of strange-achieved gold;
For this they have been thoughtful to invest
Their sons with arts and martial exercises:
When, like the bee, culling from every flower
The virtuous sweets,
Our thighs pack'd with wax, our mouths with honey,
We bring it to the hive, and, like the bees,
Are murdered for our pains. This bitter taste
Yield his engrossments to the ending father.
*Re-enter WARWICK*
Now, where is he that will not stay so long
Till his friend sickness hath determined me?
**WARWICK**
My lord, I found the prince in the next room,
Washing with kindly tears his gentle cheeks,
With such a deep demeanor in great sorrow
That tyranny, which never quaff'd but blood,
Would, by beholding him, have wash'd his knife
With gentle eye-drops. He is coming hither.
**KING HENRY IV**
But wherefore did he take away the crown?
*Re-enter PRINCE HENRY*
Lo, where he comes. Come hither to me, Harry.
Depart the chamber, leave us here alone.
*Exeunt WARWICK and the rest*
**PRINCE HENRY**
I never thought to hear you speak again.
**KING HENRY IV**
Thy wish was father, Harry, to that thought:
I stay too long by thee, I weary thee.
Dost thou so hunger for mine empty chair
That thou wilt needs invest thee with my honours
Before thy hour be ripe? O foolish youth!
Thou seek'st the greatness that will o'erwhelm thee.

Stay but a little; for my cloud of dignity
Is held from falling with so weak a wind
That it will quickly drop: my day is dim.
Thou hast stolen that which after some few hours
Were thine without offence; and at my death
Thou hast seal'd up my expectation:
Thy life did manifest thou lovedst me not,
And thou wilt have me die assured of it.
Thou hidest a thousand daggers in thy thoughts,
Which thou hast whetted on thy stony heart,
To stab at half an hour of my life.
What! canst thou not forbear me half an hour?
Then get thee gone and dig my grave thyself,
And bid the merry bells ring to thine ear
That thou art crowned, not that I am dead.
Let all the tears that should bedew my hearse
Be drops of balm to sanctify thy head:
Only compound me with forgotten dust
Give that which gave thee life unto the worms.
Pluck down my officers, break my decrees;
For now a time is come to mock at form:
Harry the Fifth is crown'd: up, vanity!
Down, royal state! all you sage counsellors, hence!
And to the English court assemble now,
From every region, apes of idleness!
Now, neighbour confines, purge you of your scum:
Have you a ruffian that will swear, drink, dance,
Revel the night, rob, murder, and commit
The oldest sins the newest kind of ways?
Be happy, he will trouble you no more;
England shall double gild his treble guilt,
England shall give him office, honour, might;
For the fifth Harry from curb'd licence plucks
The muzzle of restraint, and the wild dog
Shall flesh his tooth on every innocent.
O my poor kingdom, sick with civil blows!
When that my care could not withhold thy riots,
What wilt thou do when riot is thy care?
O, thou wilt be a wilderness again,
Peopled with wolves, thy old inhabitants!

**PRINCE HENRY**

O, pardon me, my liege! but for my tears,
The moist impediments unto my speech,
I had forestall'd this dear and deep rebuke
Ere you with grief had spoke and I had heard
The course of it so far. There is your crown;
And He that wears the crown immortally
Long guard it yours! If I affect it more
Than as your honour and as your renown,
Let me no more from this obedience rise,
Which my most inward true and duteous spirit
Teacheth, this prostrate and exterior bending.
God witness with me, when I here came in,
And found no course of breath within your majesty,
How cold it struck my heart! If I do feign,
O, let me in my present wildness die
And never live to show the incredulous world
The noble change that I have purposed!
Coming to look on you, thinking you dead,
And dead almost, my liege, to think you were,
I spake unto this crown as having sense,
And thus upbraided it: 'The care on thee depending
Hath fed upon the body of my father;

Therefore, thou best of gold art worst of gold:
Other, less fine in carat, is more precious,
Preserving life in medicine potable;
But thou, most fine, most honour'd: most renown'd,
Hast eat thy bearer up.' Thus, my most royal liege,
Accusing it, I put it on my head,
To try with it, as with an enemy
That had before my face murder'd my father,
The quarrel of a true inheritor.
But if it did infect my blood with joy,
Or swell my thoughts to any strain of pride;
If any rebel or vain spirit of mine
Did with the least affection of a welcome
Give entertainment to the might of it,
Let God for ever keep it from my head
And make me as the poorest vassal is
That doth with awe and terror kneel to it!
**KING HENRY IV**
O my son,
God put it in thy mind to take it hence,
That thou mightst win the more thy father's love,
Pleading so wisely in excuse of it!
Come hither, Harry, sit thou by my bed;
And hear, I think, the very latest counsel
That ever I shall breathe. God knows, my son,
By what by-paths and indirect crook'd ways
I met this crown; and I myself know well
How troublesome it sat upon my head.
To thee it shall descend with bitter quiet,
Better opinion, better confirmation;
For all the soil of the achievement goes
With me into the earth. It seem'd in me
But as an honour snatch'd with boisterous hand,
And I had many living to upbraid
My gain of it by their assistances;
Which daily grew to quarrel and to bloodshed,
Wounding supposed peace: all these bold fears
Thou see'st with peril I have answered;
For all my reign hath been but as a scene
Acting that argument: and now my death
Changes the mode; for what in me was purchased,
Falls upon thee in a more fairer sort;
So thou the garland wear'st successively.
Yet, though thou stand'st more sure than I could do,
Thou art not firm enough, since griefs are green;
And all my friends, which thou must make thy friends,
Have but their stings and teeth newly ta'en out;
By whose fell working I was first advanced
And by whose power I well might lodge a fear
To be again displaced: which to avoid,
I cut them off; and had a purpose now
To lead out many to the Holy Land,
Lest rest and lying still might make them look
Too near unto my state. Therefore, my Harry,
Be it thy course to busy giddy minds
With foreign quarrels; that action, hence borne out,
May waste the memory of the former days.
More would I, but my lungs are wasted so
That strength of speech is utterly denied me.
How I came by the crown, O God forgive;
And grant it may with thee in true peace live!
**PRINCE HENRY**

My gracious liege,
You won it, wore it, kept it, gave it me;
Then plain and right must my possession be:
Which I with more than with a common pain
'Gainst all the world will rightfully maintain.
*Enter Lord John of LANCASTER*
**KING HENRY IV**
Look, look, here comes my John of Lancaster.
**LANCASTER**
Health, peace, and happiness to my royal father!
**KING HENRY IV**
Thou bring'st me happiness and peace, son John;
But health, alack, with youthful wings is flown
From this bare wither'd trunk: upon thy sight
My worldly business makes a period.
Where is my Lord of Warwick?
**PRINCE HENRY**
My Lord of Warwick!
*Enter WARWICK, and others*
**KING HENRY IV**
Doth any name particular belong
Unto the lodging where I first did swoon?
**WARWICK**
'Tis call'd Jerusalem, my noble lord.
**KING HENRY IV**
Laud be to God! even there my life must end.
It hath been prophesied to me many years,
I should not die but in Jerusalem;
Which vainly I supposed the Holy Land:
But bear me to that chamber; there I'll lie;
In that Jerusalem shall Harry die.
*Exeunt*

## ACT V

### SCENE I. Gloucestershire. SHALLOW'S house.

*Enter SHALLOW, FALSTAFF, BARDOLPH, and Page*

**SHALLOW**

By cock and pie, sir, you shall not away to-night.
What, Davy, I say!

**FALSTAFF**

You must excuse me, Master Robert Shallow.

**SHALLOW**

I will not excuse you; you shall not be excused;
excuses shall not be admitted; there is no excuse
shall serve; you shall not be excused. Why, Davy!

*Enter DAVY*

**DAVY**

Here, sir.

**SHALLOW**

Davy, Davy, Davy, Davy, let me see, Davy; let me
see, Davy; let me see: yea, marry, William cook,
bid him come hither. Sir John, you shall not be excused.

**DAVY**

Marry, sir, thus; those precepts cannot be served:
and, again, sir, shall we sow the headland with wheat?

**SHALLOW**

With red wheat, Davy. But for William cook: are
there no young pigeons?

**DAVY**

Yes, sir. Here is now the smith's note for shoeing
and plough-irons.

**SHALLOW**

Let it be cast and paid. Sir John, you shall not be excused.

**DAVY**

Now, sir, a new link to the bucket must need be
had: and, sir, do you mean to stop any of William's
wages, about the sack he lost the other day at
Hinckley fair?

**SHALLOW**

A' shall answer it. Some pigeons, Davy, a couple
of short-legged hens, a joint of mutton, and any
pretty little tiny kickshaws, tell William cook.

**DAVY**

Doth the man of war stay all night, sir?

**SHALLOW**

Yea, Davy. I will use him well: a friend i' the
court is better than a penny in purse. Use his men
well, Davy; for they are arrant knaves, and will backbite.

**DAVY**

No worse than they are backbitten, sir; for they
have marvellous foul linen.

**SHALLOW**

Well conceited, Davy: about thy business, Davy.

**DAVY**

I beseech you, sir, to countenance William Visor of
Woncot against Clement Perkes of the hill.

**SHALLOW**

There is many complaints, Davy, against that Visor:
that Visor is an arrant knave, on my knowledge.

**DAVY**

I grant your worship that he is a knave, sir; but
yet, God forbid, sir, but a knave should have some
countenance at his friend's request. An honest
man, sir, is able to speak for himself, when a knave
is not. I have served your worship truly, sir,
this eight years; and if I cannot once or twice in

a quarter bear out a knave against an honest man, I
have but a very little credit with your worship. The
knave is mine honest friend, sir; therefore, I
beseech your worship, let him be countenanced.
**SHALLOW**
Go to; I say he shall have no wrong. Look about, Davy.
*Exit DAVY*
Where are you, Sir John? Come, come, come, off
with your boots. Give me your hand, Master Bardolph.
**BARDOLPH**
I am glad to see your worship.
**SHALLOW**
I thank thee with all my heart, kind
Master Bardolph: and welcome, my tall fellow.
*To the Page*
Come, Sir John.
**FALSTAFF**
I'll follow you, good Master Robert Shallow.
*Exit SHALLOW*
Bardolph, look to our horses.
*Exeunt BARDOLPH and Page*
If I were sawed into quantities, I should make four
dozen of such bearded hermits' staves as Master
Shallow. It is a wonderful thing to see the
semblable coherence of his men's spirits and his:
they, by observing of him, do bear themselves like
foolish justices; he, by conversing with them, is
turned into a justice-like serving-man: their
spirits are so married in conjunction with the
participation of society that they flock together in
consent, like so many wild-geese. If I had a suit
to Master Shallow, I would humour his men with the
imputation of being near their master: if to his
men, I would curry with Master Shallow that no man
could better command his servants. It is certain
that either wise bearing or ignorant carriage is
caught, as men take diseases, one of another:
therefore let men take heed of their company. I
will devise matter enough out of this Shallow to
keep Prince Harry in continual laughter the wearing
out of six fashions, which is four terms, or two
actions, and a' shall laugh without intervallums. O,
it is much that a lie with a slight oath and a jest
with a sad brow will do with a fellow that never
had the ache in his shoulders! O, you shall see him
laugh till his face be like a wet cloak ill laid up!
**SHALLOW**
[Within] Sir John!
**FALSTAFF**
I come, Master Shallow; I come, Master Shallow.
*Exit*
**SCENE II. Westminster. The palace.**
*Enter WARWICK and the Lord Chief-Justice, meeting*
**WARWICK**
How now, my lord chief-justice! whither away?
Lord Chief-Justice How doth the king?
**WARWICK**
Exceeding well; his cares are now all ended.
Lord Chief-Justice I hope, not dead.
**WARWICK**
He's walk'd the way of nature;
And to our purposes he lives no more.
Lord Chief-Justice I would his majesty had call'd me with him:

The service that I truly did his life
Hath left me open to all injuries.
**WARWICK**
Indeed I think the young king loves you not.
Lord Chief-Justice I know he doth not, and do arm myself
To welcome the condition of the time,
Which cannot look more hideously upon me
Than I have drawn it in my fantasy.
*Enter LANCASTER, CLARENCE, GLOUCESTER, WESTMORELAND, and others*
**WARWICK**
Here come the heavy issue of dead Harry:
O that the living Harry had the temper
Of him, the worst of these three gentlemen!
How many nobles then should hold their places
That must strike sail to spirits of vile sort!
Lord Chief-Justice O God, I fear all will be overturn'd!
**LANCASTER**
Good morrow, cousin Warwick, good morrow.
**GLOUCESTER CLARENCE**
Good morrow, cousin.
**LANCASTER**
We meet like men that had forgot to speak.
**WARWICK**
We do remember; but our argument
Is all too heavy to admit much talk.
**LANCASTER**
Well, peace be with him that hath made us heavy.
Lord Chief-Justice Peace be with us, lest we be heavier!
**GLOUCESTER**
O, good my lord, you have lost a friend indeed;
And I dare swear you borrow not that face
Of seeming sorrow, it is sure your own.
**LANCASTER**
Though no man be assured what grace to find,
You stand in coldest expectation:
I am the sorrier; would 'twere otherwise.
**CLARENCE**
Well, you must now speak Sir John Falstaff fair;
Which swims against your stream of quality.
Lord Chief-Justice Sweet princes, what I did, I did in honour,
Led by the impartial conduct of my soul:
And never shall you see that I will beg
A ragged and forestall'd remission.
If truth and upright innocency fail me,
I'll to the king my master that is dead,
And tell him who hath sent me after him.
**WARWICK**
Here comes the prince.
*Enter KING HENRY V, attended*
Lord Chief-Justice Good morrow; and God save your majesty!
**KING HENRY V**
This new and gorgeous garment, majesty,
Sits not so easy on me as you think.
Brothers, you mix your sadness with some fear:
This is the English, not the Turkish court;
Not Amurath an Amurath succeeds,
But Harry Harry. Yet be sad, good brothers,
For, by my faith, it very well becomes you:
Sorrow so royally in you appears
That I will deeply put the fashion on
And wear it in my heart: why then, be sad;
But entertain no more of it, good brothers,
Than a joint burden laid upon us all.

For me, by heaven, I bid you be assured,
I'll be your father and your brother too;
Let me but bear your love, I 'll bear your cares:
Yet weep that Harry's dead; and so will I;
But Harry lives, that shall convert those tears
By number into hours of happiness.

**Princes**

We hope no other from your majesty.

**KING HENRY V**

You all look strangely on me: and you most;
You are, I think, assured I love you not.
Lord Chief-Justice I am assured, if I be measured rightly,
Your majesty hath no just cause to hate me.

**KING HENRY V**

No!
How might a prince of my great hopes forget
So great indignities you laid upon me?
What! rate, rebuke, and roughly send to prison
The immediate heir of England! Was this easy?
May this be wash'd in Lethe, and forgotten?
Lord Chief-Justice I then did use the person of your father;
The image of his power lay then in me:
And, in the administration of his law,
Whiles I was busy for the commonwealth,
Your highness pleased to forget my place,
The majesty and power of law and justice,
The image of the king whom I presented,
And struck me in my very seat of judgment;
Whereon, as an offender to your father,
I gave bold way to my authority
And did commit you. If the deed were ill,
Be you contented, wearing now the garland,
To have a son set your decrees at nought,
To pluck down justice from your awful bench,
To trip the course of law and blunt the sword
That guards the peace and safety of your person;
Nay, more, to spurn at your most royal image
And mock your workings in a second body.
Question your royal thoughts, make the case yours;
Be now the father and propose a son,
Hear your own dignity so much profaned,
See your most dreadful laws so loosely slighted,
Behold yourself so by a son disdain'd;
And then imagine me taking your part
And in your power soft silencing your son:
After this cold considerance, sentence me;
And, as you are a king, speak in your state
What I have done that misbecame my place,
My person, or my liege's sovereignty.

**KING HENRY V**

You are right, justice, and you weigh this well;
Therefore still bear the balance and the sword:
And I do wish your honours may increase,
Till you do live to see a son of mine
Offend you and obey you, as I did.
So shall I live to speak my father's words:
'Happy am I, that have a man so bold,
That dares do justice on my proper son;
And not less happy, having such a son,
That would deliver up his greatness so
Into the hands of justice.' You did commit me:
For which, I do commit into your hand
The unstained sword that you have used to bear;

With this remembrance, that you use the same
With the like bold, just and impartial spirit
As you have done 'gainst me. There is my hand.
You shall be as a father to my youth:
My voice shall sound as you do prompt mine ear,
And I will stoop and humble my intents
To your well-practised wise directions.
And, princes all, believe me, I beseech you;
My father is gone wild into his grave,
For in his tomb lie my affections;
And with his spirit sadly I survive,
To mock the expectation of the world,
To frustrate prophecies and to raze out
Rotten opinion, who hath writ me down
After my seeming. The tide of blood in me
Hath proudly flow'd in vanity till now:
Now doth it turn and ebb back to the sea,
Where it shall mingle with the state of floods
And flow henceforth in formal majesty.
Now call we our high court of parliament:
And let us choose such limbs of noble counsel,
That the great body of our state may go
In equal rank with the best govern'd nation;
That war, or peace, or both at once, may be
As things acquainted and familiar to us;
In which you, father, shall have foremost hand.
Our coronation done, we will accite,
As I before remember'd, all our state:
And, God consigning to my good intents,
No prince nor peer shall have just cause to say,
God shorten Harry's happy life one day!
*Exeunt*
**SCENE III. Gloucestershire. SHALLOW'S orchard.**
*Enter FALSTAFF, SHALLOW, SILENCE, DAVY, BARDOLPH, and the Page*
**SHALLOW**
Nay, you shall see my orchard, where, in an arbour,
we will eat a last year's pippin of my own graffing,
with a dish of caraways, and so forth: come,
cousin Silence: and then to bed.
**FALSTAFF**
'Fore God, you have here a goodly dwelling and a rich.
**SHALLOW**
Barren, barren, barren; beggars all, beggars all,
Sir John: marry, good air. Spread, Davy; spread,
Davy; well said, Davy.
**FALSTAFF**
This Davy serves you for good uses; he is your
serving-man and your husband.
**SHALLOW**
A good varlet, a good varlet, a very good varlet,
Sir John: by the mass, I have drunk too much sack
at supper: a good varlet. Now sit down, now sit
down: come, cousin.
**SILENCE**
Ah, sirrah! quoth-a, we shall
Do nothing but eat, and make good cheer,
*Singing*
And praise God for the merry year;
When flesh is cheap and females dear,
And lusty lads roam here and there
So merrily,
And ever among so merrily.
**FALSTAFF**

There's a merry heart! Good Master Silence, I'll
give you a health for that anon.
**SHALLOW**
Give Master Bardolph some wine, Davy.
**DAVY**
Sweet sir, sit; I'll be with you anon. most sweet
sir, sit. Master page, good master page, sit.
Proface! What you want in meat, we'll have in drink:
but you must bear; the heart's all.
*Exit*
**SHALLOW**
Be merry, Master Bardolph; and, my little soldier
there, be merry.
**SILENCE**
Be merry, be merry, my wife has all;
*Singing*
For women are shrews, both short and tall:
'Tis merry in hall when beards wag all,
And welcome merry Shrove-tide.
Be merry, be merry.
**FALSTAFF**
I did not think Master Silence had been a man of
this mettle.
**SILENCE**
Who, I? I have been merry twice and once ere now.
*Re-enter DAVY*
**DAVY**
There's a dish of leather-coats for you.
*To BARDOLPH*
**SHALLOW**
Davy!
**DAVY**
Your worship! I'll be with you straight.
*To BARDOLPH*
A cup of wine, sir?
**SILENCE**
A cup of wine that's brisk and fine,
*Singing*
And drink unto the leman mine;
And a merry heart lives long-a.
**FALSTAFF**
Well said, Master Silence.
**SILENCE**
An we shall be merry, now comes in the sweet o' the night.
**FALSTAFF**
Health and long life to you, Master Silence.
**SILENCE**
Fill the cup, and let it come;
*Singing*
I'll pledge you a mile to the bottom.
**SHALLOW**
Honest Bardolph, welcome: if thou wantest any
thing, and wilt not call, beshrew thy heart.
Welcome, my little tiny thief.
*To the Page*
And welcome indeed too. I'll drink to Master
Bardolph, and to all the cavaleros about London.
**DAVY**
I hove to see London once ere I die.
**BARDOLPH**
An I might see you there, Davy,--
**SHALLOW**

By the mass, you'll crack a quart together, ha!
Will you not, Master Bardolph?
**BARDOLPH**
Yea, sir, in a pottle-pot.
**SHALLOW**
By God's liggens, I thank thee: the knave will
stick by thee, I can assure thee that. A' will not
out; he is true bred.
**BARDOLPH**
And I'll stick by him, sir.
**SHALLOW**
Why, there spoke a king. Lack nothing: be merry.
*Knocking within*
Look who's at door there, ho! who knocks?
*Exit DAVY*
**FALSTAFF**
Why, now you have done me right.
*To SILENCE, seeing him take off a bumper*
**SILENCE**
[Singing]
Do me right,
And dub me knight: Samingo.
Is't not so?
**FALSTAFF**
'Tis so.
**SILENCE**
Is't so? Why then, say an old man can do somewhat.
*Re-enter DAVY*
**DAVY**
An't please your worship, there's one Pistol come
from the court with news.
**FALSTAFF**
From the court! let him come in.
*Enter PISTOL*
How now, Pistol!
**PISTOL**
Sir John, God save you!
**FALSTAFF**
What wind blew you hither, Pistol?
**PISTOL**
Not the ill wind which blows no man to good. Sweet
knight, thou art now one of the greatest men in this realm.
**SILENCE**
By'r lady, I think a' be, but goodman Puff of Barson.
**PISTOL**
Puff!
Puff in thy teeth, most recreant coward base!
Sir John, I am thy Pistol and thy friend,
And helter-skelter have I rode to thee,
And tidings do I bring and lucky joys
And golden times and happy news of price.
**FALSTAFF**
I pray thee now, deliver them like a man of this world.
**PISTOL**
A foutre for the world and worldlings base!
I speak of Africa and golden joys.
**FALSTAFF**
O base Assyrian knight, what is thy news?
Let King Cophetua know the truth thereof.
**SILENCE**
And Robin Hood, Scarlet, and John.
*Singing*
**PISTOL**

Shall dunghill curs confront the Helicons?
And shall good news be baffled?
Then, Pistol, lay thy head in Furies' lap.
**SILENCE**
Honest gentleman, I know not your breeding.
**PISTOL**
Why then, lament therefore.
**SHALLOW**
Give me pardon, sir: if, sir, you come with news
from the court, I take it there's but two ways,
either to utter them, or to conceal them. I am,
sir, under the king, in some authority.
**PISTOL**
Under which king, Besonian? speak, or die.
**SHALLOW**
Under King Harry.
**PISTOL**
Harry the Fourth? or Fifth?
**SHALLOW**
Harry the Fourth.
**PISTOL**
A foutre for thine office!
Sir John, thy tender lambkin now is king;
Harry the Fifth's the man. I speak the truth:
When Pistol lies, do this; and fig me, like
The bragging Spaniard.
**FALSTAFF**
What, is the old king dead?
**PISTOL**
As nail in door: the things I speak are just.
**FALSTAFF**
Away, Bardolph! saddle my horse. Master Robert
Shallow, choose what office thou wilt in the land,
'tis thine. Pistol, I will double-charge thee with dignities.
**BARDOLPH**
O joyful day!
I would not take a knighthood for my fortune.
**PISTOL**
What! I do bring good news.
**FALSTAFF**
Carry Master Silence to bed. Master Shallow, my
Lord Shallow,--be what thou wilt; I am fortune's
steward--get on thy boots: we'll ride all night.
O sweet Pistol! Away, Bardolph!
*Exit BARDOLPH*
Come, Pistol, utter more to me; and withal devise
something to do thyself good. Boot, boot, Master
Shallow: I know the young king is sick for me. Let
us take any man's horses; the laws of England are at
my commandment. Blessed are they that have been my
friends; and woe to my lord chief-justice!
**PISTOL**
Let vultures vile seize on his lungs also!
'Where is the life that late I led?' say they:
Why, here it is; welcome these pleasant days!
*Exeunt*
**SCENE IV. London. A street.**
*Enter Beadles, dragging in HOSTESS QUICKLY and DOLL TEARSHEET*
**MISTRESS QUICKLY**
No, thou arrant knave; I would to God that I might
die, that I might have thee hanged: thou hast
drawn my shoulder out of joint.
**First Beadle**

The constables have delivered her over to me; and
she shall have whipping-cheer enough, I warrant
her: there hath been a man or two lately killed about her.

**DOLL TEARSHEET**

Nut-hook, nut-hook, you lie. Come on; I 'll tell
thee what, thou damned tripe-visaged rascal, an
the child I now go with do miscarry, thou wert
better thou hadst struck thy mother, thou
paper-faced villain.

**MISTRESS QUICKLY**

O the Lord, that Sir John were come! he would make
this a bloody day to somebody. But I pray God the
fruit of her womb miscarry!

**First Beadle**

If it do, you shall have a dozen of cushions again;
you have but eleven now. Come, I charge you both go
with me; for the man is dead that you and Pistol
beat amongst you.

**DOLL TEARSHEET**

I'll tell you what, you thin man in a censer, I
will have you as soundly swinged for this,--you
blue-bottle rogue, you filthy famished correctioner,
if you be not swinged, I'll forswear half-kirtles.

**First Beadle**

Come, come, you she knight-errant, come.

**MISTRESS QUICKLY**

O God, that right should thus overcome might!
Well, of sufferance comes ease.

**DOLL TEARSHEET**

Come, you rogue, come; bring me to a justice.

**MISTRESS QUICKLY**

Ay, come, you starved blood-hound.

**DOLL TEARSHEET**

Goodman death, goodman bones!

**MISTRESS QUICKLY**

Thou atomy, thou!

**DOLL TEARSHEET**

Come, you thin thing; come you rascal.

**First Beadle**

Very well.

*Exeunt*

**SCENE V. A public place near Westminster Abbey.**

*Enter two Grooms, strewing rushes*

**First Groom**

More rushes, more rushes.

**Second Groom**

The trumpets have sounded twice.

**First Groom**

'Twill be two o'clock ere they come from the
coronation: dispatch, dispatch.

*Exeunt*

*Enter FALSTAFF, SHALLOW, PISTOL, BARDOLPH, and Page*

**FALSTAFF**

Stand here by me, Master Robert Shallow; I will
make the king do you grace: I will leer upon him as
a' comes by; and do but mark the countenance that he
will give me.

**PISTOL**

God bless thy lungs, good knight.

**FALSTAFF**

Come here, Pistol; stand behind me. O, if I had had
time to have made new liveries, I would have
bestowed the thousand pound I borrowed of you. But

'tis no matter; this poor show doth better: this
doth infer the zeal I had to see him.
**SHALLOW**
It doth so.
**FALSTAFF**
It shows my earnestness of affection,--
**SHALLOW**
It doth so.
**FALSTAFF**
My devotion,--
**SHALLOW**
It doth, it doth, it doth.
**FALSTAFF**
As it were, to ride day and night; and not to
deliberate, not to remember, not to have patience
to shift me,--
**SHALLOW**
It is best, certain.
**FALSTAFF**
But to stand stained with travel, and sweating with
desire to see him; thinking of nothing else,
putting all affairs else in oblivion, as if there
were nothing else to be done but to see him.
**PISTOL**
'Tis 'semper idem,' for 'obsque hoc nihil est:'
'tis all in every part.
**SHALLOW**
'Tis so, indeed.
**PISTOL**
My knight, I will inflame thy noble liver,
And make thee rage.
Thy Doll, and Helen of thy noble thoughts,
Is in base durance and contagious prison;
Haled thither
By most mechanical and dirty hand:
Rouse up revenge from ebon den with fell
Alecto's snake,
For Doll is in. Pistol speaks nought but truth.
**FALSTAFF**
I will deliver her.
*Shouts within, and the trumpets sound*
**PISTOL**
There roar'd the sea, and trumpet-clangor sounds.
*Enter KING HENRY V and his train, the Lord Chief- Justice among them*
**FALSTAFF**
God save thy grace, King Hal! my royal Hal!
**PISTOL**
The heavens thee guard and keep, most royal imp of fame!
**FALSTAFF**
God save thee, my sweet boy!
**KING HENRY IV**
My lord chief-justice, speak to that vain man.
Lord Chief-Justice Have you your wits? know you what 'tis to speak?
**FALSTAFF**
My king! my Jove! I speak to thee, my heart!
**KING HENRY IV**
I know thee not, old man: fall to thy prayers;
How ill white hairs become a fool and jester!
I have long dream'd of such a kind of man,
So surfeit-swell'd, so old and so profane;
But, being awaked, I do despise my dream.
Make less thy body hence, and more thy grace;
Leave gormandizing; know the grave doth gape

For thee thrice wider than for other men.
Reply not to me with a fool-born jest:
Presume not that I am the thing I was;
For God doth know, so shall the world perceive,
That I have turn'd away my former self;
So will I those that kept me company.
When thou dost hear I am as I have been,
Approach me, and thou shalt be as thou wast,
The tutor and the feeder of my riots:
Till then, I banish thee, on pain of death,
As I have done the rest of my misleaders,
Not to come near our person by ten mile.
For competence of life I will allow you,
That lack of means enforce you not to evil:
And, as we hear you do reform yourselves,
We will, according to your strengths and qualities,
Give you advancement. Be it your charge, my lord,
To see perform'd the tenor of our word. Set on.
*Exeunt KING HENRY V, & c*
**FALSTAFF**
Master Shallow, I owe you a thousand pound.
**SHALLOW**
Yea, marry, Sir John; which I beseech you to let me
have home with me.
**FALSTAFF**
That can hardly be, Master Shallow. Do not you
grieve at this; I shall be sent for in private to
him: look you, he must seem thus to the world:
fear not your advancements; I will be the man yet
that shall make you great.
**SHALLOW**
I cannot well perceive how, unless you should give
me your doublet and stuff me out with straw. I
beseech you, good Sir John, let me have five hundred
of my thousand.
**FALSTAFF**
Sir, I will be as good as my word: this that you
heard was but a colour.
**SHALLOW**
A colour that I fear you will die in, Sir John.
**FALSTAFF**
Fear no colours: go with me to dinner: come,
Lieutenant Pistol; come, Bardolph: I shall be sent
for soon at night.
*Re-enter Prince John of LANCASTER, the Lord Chief-Justice; Officers with them*
Lord Chief-Justice Go, carry Sir John Falstaff to the Fleet:
Take all his company along with him.
**FALSTAFF**
My lord, my lord,--
Lord Chief-Justice I cannot now speak: I will hear you soon.
Take them away.
**PISTOL**
Si fortune me tormenta, spero contenta.
*Exeunt all but PRINCE JOHN and the Lord Chief-Justice*
**LANCASTER**
I like this fair proceeding of the king's:
He hath intent his wonted followers
Shall all be very well provided for;
But all are banish'd till their conversations
Appear more wise and modest to the world.
Lord Chief-Justice And so they are.
**LANCASTER**

The king hath call'd his parliament, my lord.
Lord Chief-Justice He hath.
**LANCASTER**
I will lay odds that, ere this year expire,
We bear our civil swords and native fire
As far as France: I beard a bird so sing,
Whose music, to my thinking, pleased the king.
Come, will you hence?
*Exeunt*
EPILOGUE
*Spoken by a Dancer*
First my fear; then my courtesy; last my speech.
My fear is, your displeasure; my courtesy, my duty;
and my speech, to beg your pardons. If you look
for a good speech now, you undo me: for what I have
to say is of mine own making; and what indeed I
should say will, I doubt, prove mine own marring.
But to the purpose, and so to the venture. Be it
known to you, as it is very well, I was lately here
in the end of a displeasing play, to pray your
patience for it and to promise you a better. I
meant indeed to pay you with this; which, if like an
ill venture it come unluckily home, I break, and
you, my gentle creditors, lose. Here I promised you
I would be and here I commit my body to your
mercies: bate me some and I will pay you some and,
as most debtors do, promise you infinitely.
If my tongue cannot entreat you to acquit me, will
you command me to use my legs? and yet that were but
light payment, to dance out of your debt. But a
good conscience will make any possible satisfaction,
and so would I. All the gentlewomen here have
forgiven me: if the gentlemen will not, then the
gentlemen do not agree with the gentlewomen, which
was never seen before in such an assembly.
One word more, I beseech you. If you be not too
much cloyed with fat meat, our humble author will
continue the story, with Sir John in it, and make
you merry with fair Katharine of France: where, for
any thing I know, Falstaff shall die of a sweat,
unless already a' be killed with your hard
opinions; for Oldcastle died a martyr, and this is
not the man. My tongue is weary; when my legs are
too, I will bid you good night: and so kneel down
before you; but, indeed, to pray for the queen.

Made in the USA
Middletown, DE
31 August 2017